TWO TRUTHS AND A LIE

OTHER MYSTERIES BY APRIL HENRY

Girl, Stolen

The Night She Disappeared

The Girl Who Was Supposed to Die

The Girl I Used to Be

Count All Her Bones

The Lonely Dead

Run, Hide, Fight Back

The Girl in the White Van

Playing with Fire

Eyes of the Forest

THE POINT LAST SEEN SERIES

The Body in the Woods

Blood Will Tell

TWO TRUTHS AND A LIE

April Henry

Christy Ottaviano Books

LITTLE, BROWN AND COMPANY
New York Boston

Copyright © 2022 by April Henry
Map art by David Lindroth

Cover image of motel © Sabrina Janelle Gordon/Shutterstock.com.
Cover image of face © AlohaHawaii/Shutterstock.com.
Cover image of broken glass © Deyan Georgiev/Shutterstock.com.
Cover design by Karina Granda
Cover copyright © 2022 by Hachette Book Group, Inc.

Christy Ottaviano Books
Hachette Book Group
1290 Avenue of the Americas, New York, NY 10104
Visit us at LBYR.com

First Edition: May 2022

Christy Ottaviano Books is an imprint of Little, Brown and Company. The Christy Ottaviano Books name and logo are trademarks of Hachette Book Group, Inc.

The publisher is not responsible for websites (or their content) that are not owned by the publisher.

Library of Congress Cataloging-in-Publication Data
Names: Henry, April, author.
Title: Two truths and a lie / April Henry.
Description: First edition. | New York ; Boston : Christy Ottaviano Books/Little, Brown and Company, 2022. | Audience: Ages 12–18. | Summary: "When a troupe of theater students get stranded in a creepy old motel during a blizzard, they play a foreboding game of truth and lies that leads to real danger when a murderer is discovered in their midst." —Provided by publisher.
Identifiers: LCCN 2021040273 | ISBN 9780316323338 (hardcover) | ISBN 9780316323574 (ebook)
Subjects: CYAC: Murder—Fiction. | Theater—Fiction. | Hotels, motels, etc.—Fiction. | LCGFT: Novels. | Thrillers (Fiction)
Classification: LCC PZ7.H39356 Tw 2022 | DDC [Fic]—dc23
LC record available at https://lccn.loc.gov/2021040273

ISBNs: 978-0-316-32333-8 (hardcover), 978-0-316-32357-4 (ebook)

Printed in the United States of America

LSC-C

Printing 1, 2022

In February 2019, a group of strangers trapped by a blizzard at a literacy festival barely managed to escape.

———•———

This book is dedicated to that merry band, which included literacy expert Bernadette Dwyer, author Barbara Boroson, and author Ann Marie Stephens. The biggest thanks of all goes to our fearless leader, Sarah Rose Sell, a teacher who saw my plight on Twitter, offered to rescue as many as would fit in her car, and then ended up trapped with us far from her home (and her newborn). "I was a stranger, and you took me in."

"Monsters are real, and
ghosts are real, too.
They live inside us, and
sometimes they win."

—STEPHEN KING, FROM A PREFACE
TO *THE SHINING*

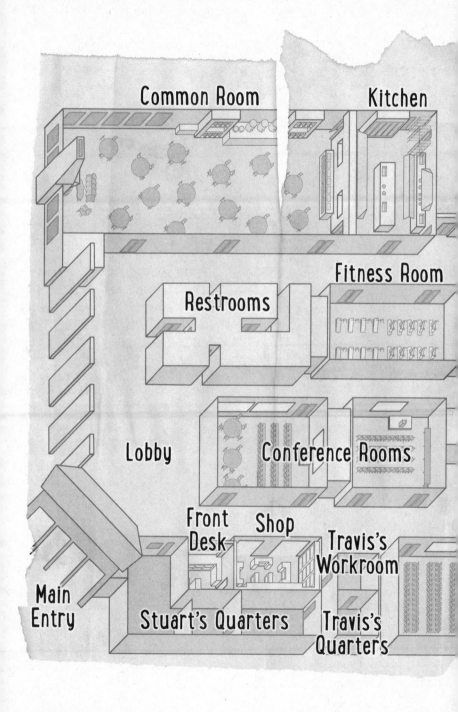

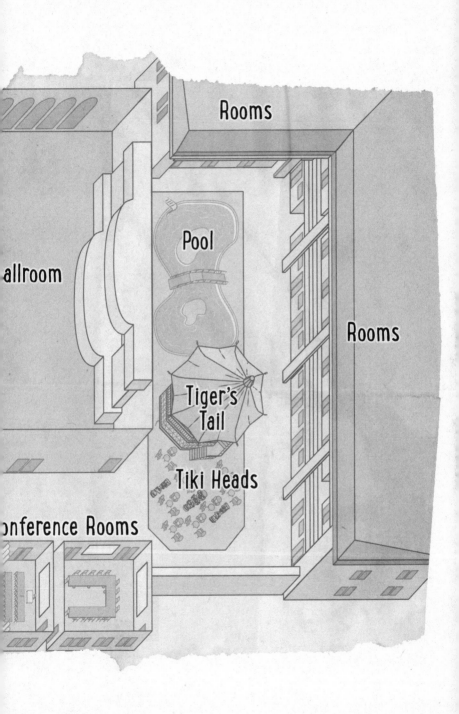

TWO
TRUTHS
AND A
LIE

LOOK WHERE YOU WANT TO GO

Friday, 2:40 PM

"SHOTGUN!" I SHOUT AS MRS. MCELROY PULLS UP TO THE CURB.

Through some mysterious magic known only to her, Mrs. McElroy has been able to wheedle use of a school-district vehicle this weekend. Normally only the athletic teams—we theater kids lump them together as "sports ball"—get that kind of support. So we'll be traveling to the theater competition at the state capital in style.

That is, if your idea of style is a tan minivan.

"No fair, Mom!" Raven pouts. The nickname got started last fall after I brought in treats to make the week prior to opening night (better known as Hell Week) more bearable.

"Hey, the adults always sit in the front seat," Adam

says, opening the back gate. All five of us try to jam our suitcases into the small luggage space, until he takes charge.

As Adam fits all the suitcases together like puzzle pieces, something soft and cold dots the tip of my nose. I look up. Flakes are falling from the concrete-gray sky.

With a grin, my best friend, Min, tips her head back and sticks out her tongue to catch one.

Maybe I look anxious, because Adam says, "Don't worry, Nell," as he slots a backpack into a gap. "It won't stick. The forecast says just a few flurries."

We haven't gotten much snow this winter, at least by Midwest standards. My family moved here from Los Angeles a little over a year ago, so the snow is still sort of a novelty. I had imagined pristine drifts, snowmen, and snowball fights. The reality has been a lot less picturesque. In the corner of the parking lot, just like all parking lots around here, there's a head-high, dingy gray pile. With each passing week, it gets a little dirtier and a little smaller. Now it's spring, at least on paper.

Beep! Beep! Mrs. McElroy honks the horn to hurry us up. Adam slides open the side door and then scrambles in, contorting his long legs to sit in the far corner. Everyone else follows. I pull the door shut and then take my seat in the front.

Min starts immediately playing the *Hamilton* sound-track on her phone. While she has by far the best singing voice, we all sing along at full volume and with dramatic gestures. Everyone's excited about competing and even about the trip to the capital. To them, it's a big city. The nearest actual big city is Chicago, and that's the better part of a day's drive away. As Mrs. McElroy pulls out of the parking lot, we ignore the stares from the kids waiting for their parents or the bus.

Or maybe we don't. All of us love an audience. It's kind of a given if you're an actor.

"I'm not sure one minivan can contain all this energy," Mrs. McElroy says in a pause between songs. But she's grinning when she says it.

We all live, sleep, and breathe theater. For many of us, theater is our truest family, sometimes our only family. Theater is the place where being weird is embraced, not shunned. We know what we're like when we're stripped of everything, both literally and figuratively—and yet we still love one another.

Six hours later, it's become clear that the forecast was wrong.

As the hours have passed and the snow kept falling, the minivan has gotten quiet. The weather app said something about the polar vortex shifting unexpectedly.

And then we lost service.

By that time we were surrounded by acres of flat farm-land, halfway between home and the capital and with no good choices. But we had already come so far. And the snow wasn't falling that hard. We decided to continue.

Which was clearly a mistake.

For the millionth time, I check my phone. *No service.* Knowing theoretically that some areas don't have cell service is way different than experiencing it yourself.

We're already over six hours into what was supposed to be a four-hour drive and still have at least a hundred miles to go. Mrs. McElroy is holding the steering wheel so tightly that her gnarled fingers are nearly as white as the world outside the windows.

White, dancing flakes falling through the darkness. White snow-covered empty fields stretching endlessly on either side of us. The headlights barely illuminate the faint black ruts in the white that are the only sign we're still on the highway.

A half hour ago, the semi we'd followed for miles turned off. Now we're all alone, a tiny boat in the middle of a vast ocean.

A yellow light flickers in the sky ahead of us. As we drive underneath an overpass, I tip back my head to read the flashing sign. BLIZZARD WARNING. BLIZZARD WARNING. BLIZZARD WARNING. It wasn't until I moved here that I learned that a blizzard isn't just snow—you also need at least thirty-five-mile-an-hour winds.

I turn to look behind me. Instead of everyone staring tensely out the windows, they all seem to be asleep. Asleep!

Min is the only one awake. She's in the back seat next to Adam, playing a game on her phone. Back when we still had service and the snow was light, she was on Yelp, checking out coffee shops along our route. But even then Mrs. McElroy insisted there would be no detours or delays.

In the middle row of seats, Raven sleeps with her head against Jermaine's broad shoulder. It's odd to see her still. Normally, Raven puts the drama in drama club.

Jermaine's new to acting. On a whim, he tried out for a part in the winter play. A wide receiver, acting? But he's been good, as natural as he is on the field. He likes the behind-the-scenes stuff, too, like the lingo and the little tricks we use to make things look real. Plus having half the football team in the audience on opening night was a nice bonus.

A certain tension in the lines of Raven's and Jermaine's bodies makes me think they're both pretending to be dozing. It gives their current cuddling a certain plausible deniability. For weeks, Raven's been angling to get Jermaine to notice her. Now one of her hands is even resting on his thigh.

Mrs. McElroy's low voice interrupts my thoughts. "It's getting harder and harder to see." Her shoulders are hunched, her head jutting forward like a turtle's. The fear in her voice unsettles me even more than the snow. Mrs. McElroy isn't afraid of anything.

"Maybe try the brights?" I touch the gold tragedy/comedy-mask necklace my moms gave me on my sixteenth birthday. It feels like it brings me luck, so onstage, I tuck it in a pocket or my bra. And right now, we could use a little luck.

When Mrs. McElroy flicks the switch, the road totally disappears. All we can see is a swarm of flakes rushing at us. With a gasp, she quickly switches the lights back to the regular setting.

Suddenly, there's a sickening, sliding sensation as our back wheels lose purchase. Startled awake, Raven shrieks. Just when I think we're going to crash, the minivan straightens out.

"Sorry, everybody." Mrs. McElroy takes a deep breath. "I've got to remember to be very gentle with the brakes."

"In driver's ed," Adam says from the back, "they tell us to look where you want to go, not at what you're afraid of. I guess you subconsciously drive toward whatever you are focused on."

Raven's voice trembles. "If it were me driving right now, the only way that idea would work would be if I closed my eyes!" She clutches Jermaine.

"Shh, babe." His voice is soft. "It'll be okay."

"I can't keep driving in this," Mrs. McElroy says. "Everyone keep an eye out. As soon as we see any kind of hotel or town, I'm getting off this road."

BEHAVE YOURSELVES
Friday, 8:39 PM

FINALLY, A SIGN APPEARS IN THE DARKNESS. "THAT SAYS 'LODG-
ing ahead.'" I squint, trying to make out the words.
"'Travel Inn and Out.'" The pun makes me wince.

A ticking sound fills the van as Mrs. McElroy puts on
her turn signal like there's someone to see it. The minivan
slows to a crawl as she takes the exit. The ruts of other cars
are now just suggestions.

"There!" I call out. Part of the lighted sign is dead, so it
just reads TRAVEL INN.

We turn into the parking lot, which holds only a big
rig and a handful of cars. Every time the tires slide, Raven
squeals. Jermaine is now leaning away from her.

Light from the lobby reflects on the snow, but the rest of the motel looks dark.

"I don't think we'll have any trouble getting rooms," Adam says as Mrs. McElroy stops under an overhang.

"Maybe it's not even open." Min's mouth twists.

"But the sign's lit up." I press my face against the cold window. "And I think I see someone inside."

"I hope they have a restaurant," Jermaine says. "I'm starving."

Adam reaches past him to touch Mrs. McElroy's shoulder. "Thank you for getting us here safely."

Everyone echoes him as Raven opens the sliding door. People start climbing out.

When I open my door, a gust yanks it out of my hand. The air is so cold it feels like it's pulling my lungs inside out.

Shivering, I gather with the rest at the back of the mini-van. Even under the overhang, there are several inches of snow. After grabbing my suitcase, I follow the others inside. There's a small vestibule with doors on either side, probably to keep weather like this out.

As soon as she's through the second set of doors, Raven drops to her knees and makes a show of kissing the tile floor, like she's been lost at sea.

Behind her, Min and I exchange an eye roll, before she clasps her hands and looks heavenward. "Thank you, Jesus! Thank you!" Then Min snorts in my ear as she gives me a hug.

The clerk looks at us with his head tilted. He's tall and thin, a pale middle-aged guy with receding black hair.

"Seeking refuge from the storm?" He does an admirable job of keeping a straight face at our antics.

Mrs. McElroy moves ahead of us as Jermaine helps Raven to her feet.

"Good evening, Mr., um"—she squints at his name tag—"Mr. Nowell. Do you have any rooms with more than two beds?"

"Just call me Stuart. And I'm afraid all our rooms have just two queens or one king."

As he's speaking, a man dressed in coveralls and with a graying mullet pushes a yellow janitor's cart out of an unmarked door. His mustache and goatee form a square around his lips, reminding me of a nutcracker soldier. Wordlessly, he starts to mop up the slushy snow we've tracked in with us. When he turns his head, the side of his face catches the light, and I flinch. On his temple is a dent about the size of a Brazil nut.

Mrs. McElroy turns to count heads as she pulls her wallet from her purse. "I've got three girls and two boys, so I guess we'll just take four rooms. Adam and Jermaine, you'll room together. I'll let you girls decide which one of you is going to get a room by themselves. And I'll take a room."

"Wait a minute." Raven puts her hands on her hips. "Why do you automatically get a room to yourself?"

"Because I'm old and cranky, that's why. Besides, I don't see any of you pulling out your credit cards." She holds up hers. "If you want to pay for it, feel free to upgrade yourself. I'll be lucky if the school district reimburses me before I retire."

When no one says anything, Mrs. McElroy finishes registering us. It's kind of a given that Min and I will share a room. We've been best friends since I moved here. I expect Raven to protest that she's scared to be alone—because Raven protests everything—but she keeps still. I wonder if she's hoping to take advantage of it later.

Instead of card keys, we get actual metal keys, which I guess shouldn't be a surprise. This place seems to exist in a time before we were born.

Jermaine looks up from his phone. "What's the Wi-Fi password?" he asks Stuart.

"*TravelInn&Out*, all one word, with an ampersand." Everyone starts typing it into their phones, relieved to reconnect to the real world.

"That reminds me," Mrs. McElroy says. "You all need to get in touch with your parents to let them know you're safe."

"What if our calls can't go through?" Min waves her phone.

Stuart pushes one of those cordless phones that looks like a TV clicker toward her. "You can use the motel phone for quick calls, but I'd do it soon. I wouldn't be surprised if the lines go down later."

I just send my moms a short e-mail. I don't want to spend a bunch of time reassuring them, not when everything is okay now.

As Min picks up the handset, Mrs. McElroy sighs. "I'll need to call our original hotel and the conference chair and tell them we're not going to make it."

"Maybe we can still get up early and drive in tomorrow," Jermaine says. "That way we won't miss that much of the contest."

Adam looks up from his phone. "No one's going anyplace. There's more snow in the forecast. And after a twenty-three-car accident, they're shutting down the highway."

"But the competition was supposed to be our moment!" Raven says. "You're juniors. For us seniors, there won't be another chance. This was our thing"—her voice breaks as she repeats the words—"our one thing, and it's ruined."

Jermaine puts his arm around her shoulders. "Maybe they'll reschedule."

Which they won't. Everyone knows that. He's thinking like the football player he is. Sports are the most important thing at our school and in our state. Drama doesn't even come in second. Or third or fourth. Maybe thirteenth.

Min is now using the old phone to call her parents. She actually has to raise her voice to be heard over the howling of the wind.

Hearing it makes me shiver, even though my coat's still

zipped all the way up. Now that we're inside a building, I should be feeling safe and warm. But it seems like forces bigger than us, bigger than this sprawling deserted motel, are at work. As if they want to pry the roof off this place like peeling back the lid on a tin can.

Stuart slides a laminated piece of paper toward us. "You should check out this map before you go to your rooms. This place can be like a maze. It was built in the fifties, but then it was added on to about ten years back, so the room numbers are a bit confusing. I'll be putting you guys in rooms that start with four, but they're actually on the second floor." His finger traces a path. "To get to the elevator, you'll need to go past the meeting rooms, the bar, and the pool."

While a few of us give the map a cursory glance, Adam scans the large lobby, empty except for us and the guy who is now finishing up the mopping. "Why is this motel so big? We only saw a few lights when we pulled in."

Stuart presses his lips together for a second. "My parents tried to turn this place into a convention center, but it never really took off. That's why we've got meeting rooms and even a ballroom." He brightens. "But the common room has some board games you kids might enjoy. It's also where we serve breakfast."

"Speaking of breakfast..." Jermaine puts his hand on his stomach. "Is there a place we can grab some dinner?"

Stuart shakes his head. "We only serve lunch or dinner

when we're catering events. Otherwise, there's just a continental breakfast from seven to ten on weekends. But we have a little store in the next room, plus a vending machine in the common room."

I raise my hand. "And I packed some food in my luggage."

"Ooh!" Raven sidles closer. "What you got for us, Mom?"

Now it doesn't sound like much. "Mandarin oranges. And a bunch of mini candy bars."

My paltry offerings aren't enough to stop everyone from checking out the store. I follow them into a plain beige room. On two sides are wall-mounted shelves, with a cooler full of soda on the third.

Aside from Cup Noodles and a few tiny containers of microwavable ravioli, the shelves hold very little that can be thought of as dinner material. Instead it's a junk-food paradise: red Twizzlers, orange cheese popcorn, Dots, Oreos, Nerds, pretzels, Mike and Ikes, Twix, Snickers, Kit Kats, and Hostess fruit pies.

People are filling their arms when Raven leans close to a printout posted on the wall and lets out a shriek.

"Look at the prices! Five dollars for a little can of Pringles!"

Adam shrugs. He has only a Snickers. "Don't you remember economics? It's the law of supply and demand. We're just lucky that Stuart guy hasn't jacked up the prices now that he knows he has a captive audience."

Everyone begins to reluctantly follow Adam's example, keeping only a couple of items and returning the others to the shelves. I end up with ravioli and a fruit pie.

Mrs. McElroy comes in and plucks the last chicken-flavored Cup Noodles from the shelves. "After I moved the van, I talked to the hotel, but I couldn't get hold of the conference chair. It just went straight to voice mail. Now I'm going to eat this in my room, and then I'm going to sleep. I expect you guys to behave yourselves. I do not want to have to spend time explaining myself to your parents."

"We'll be good," Min says. "We promise!"

"Mm-hmm." Mrs. McElroy raises a skeptical eyebrow. "I trust that none of you is going to wake me up or do anything that causes me to be awoken. I'm taking a sleeping pill and putting on my sleep mask, and I plan to get up just before they stop serving breakfast."

"Yes, ma'am," Jermaine says, while the rest of us nod or mutter agreement. We all love Mrs. McElroy, which is why we will all police one another. There's nothing worse than disappointing her.

After she leaves, Min glances out at the dim lobby. "This place feels creepy."

"Shh, he'll hear you," I say. Min's right, but I don't want Stuart to overhear.

Raven shrugs. "We're only going to be here one night. What difference does it make?"

After leaving the little store, we pay for the items at the

front desk. Stuart rings up our purchases with an impassive face, so impassive I wonder if he heard Min. The janitor or handyman or whatever he was is gone, and the floor is as clean as if we had never tramped over it.

Dragging our suitcases behind us, we're heading to the elevator with our packages of sugary, fatty goodness when the door to the foyer opens, letting in a gust of icy air.

And another group of teens.

VERY META

Friday, 8:57 PM

HURRYING IN FRONT OF THE STUDENTS IS A SHORT BLACK GUY IN his forties. I figure he's their teacher. His head is shaved, and he's wearing a bulky down coat.

Speaking with a strong southern accent, he points at the phone on the counter. "Hey, man, I need to call a tow truck. My car slid off the road not far from here. Luckily these kids came along and gave me a ride."

Okay, so he's not their teacher.

Stuart gives him an amused look. "Nobody's gonna come out in weather like this. You'll be lucky if they can tow it by Monday."

The rest of the group has reached the counter. A tall

guy claps the man on the back. "You're just lucky we came along when we did, Linus." The speaker has a heart-shaped face, blue eyes accented by the wings of black brows, and pale skin that sets off his red lips.

Min sees me staring and elbows me. "He looks like a vampire," she whispers.

"He can bite me anytime," I whisper back. He's definitely my type. My type in books or movies, that is. In real life, I have lots of friends who are boys, but I've never had an actual boyfriend, unless you count one week of seventh grade.

Other than Linus, there are five people in the new group. Vampire Boy, two more guys, and two girls. One guy is a little older than the rest, maybe in his early twenties. Too old for high school, too young to be a parent. The teacher?

Raven claps her hands. "Oh my God, are you going to the state drama competition, too?"

They all turn toward us. "Well—" the guy who's barely an adult starts.

"Actually"—Vampire Boy overrides him—"we're on our way to the state robotics competition."

"Yup!" a slender girl with the most amazing long red curls chimes in. "Robotics." She slips her arm around Vampire Boy's waist, and my heart sinks a little, until she transfers it to the slightly older guy's shoulders. "At least that's where we *were* going, right, Mr. Ewing?"

His face colors as he ducks away from her arm. "Please, Maeve, just call me Oscar when we're not at school. I'm still in college, and Mr. Ewing always makes me think of my dad."

"If your robotics competition is at the capital," Adam says, "the news is saying that the highway is closed at least until tomorrow afternoon."

"I'm not sorry," Oscar says. "Because I'm still shaking. I need some time to recuperate from that crazy driving."

While he's speaking, Linus, the man whose car slid off the road, takes his key from Stuart. "Thanks again, guys!" he says, giving the new group a little wave before walking off.

"He doesn't even have a suitcase," Min observes.

"The whole frame of his car was knocked out of whack," Vampire Boy says. "He kept trying to force open the trunk, but he couldn't."

While Oscar and Stuart are having a conversation about rates and beds, Maeve runs her eyes up and down Jermaine appreciatively. "So you guys are actors, huh?"

Raven steps closer to him and puts her hand on his arm. "Yup. I'm Raven, and this is Jermaine."

We all introduce ourselves. Vampire Boy points a thumb at himself. "I'm Knox."

"As in 'school of hard,'" purrs Maeve, bumping him with her hip.

"And I'm Valeria." A black-haired girl wiggles her

fingers. Her dark eyes are accented with so much liner and extra lashes it's a wonder she can hold them open. I catch Min eyeing her. Valeria's definitely her type. Tiny, big-eyed, and ultrafeminine. Despite the chilly day, she's even wearing a dress.

The remaining guy is Dev. He has thick black eyebrows and a watchful expression. Compared with the others, he seems relatively restrained.

"I'm Raven. And we just wrapped *Our Town*," Raven says. "I played Emily, and Adam here was the Stage Manager." Adam gives the new group a salute. "That's what the character is actually called," Raven clarifies. "Stage Manager. He's never actually given a name."

"Those are the two lead roles," I say, in case the others can't tell from her tone. "The play's like a hundred years old, but it's very meta—there's no props, and the Stage Manager interrupts and comments and even talks directly to the audience."

"Thanks for the explanation," Knox says with a grin that pierces my heart. "So were you guys going to perform it at the competition?"

"Only a couple of groups are doing full plays," Adam says. "We're doing smaller things." He ticks them off on his fingers. "We've got people competing in monologues, duet acting, small-group improv, solo musical, and duet musical. Min here is our secret weapon for any of the musical categories."

"And there's a technical challenge," I add. I'm participating in some of the other categories, but everyone, most especially me, knows that I'm not nearly as good an actor as I would like to be. Lighting, props, makeup, costumes—all those behind-the-scenes things are where I really shine.

Dev looks interested. "What does a technical challenge involve?"

"Focus a spotlight in an unusual shape, tie knots, quickly change someone's costume, shift props, that kind of stuff. And it's all timed. What do you guys have to do for your robotics competition?"

"We'll be given a challenge and a time limit to figure it out. Like"—Knox hunts for an example—"like maybe we'll have to build a little robot that can push around a golf ball and alter direction on its own without anyone controlling it." He's clearly their leader. Everyone is watching him raptly, even the student teacher, as if he's saying something they don't already know. "Just competing looks great on college applications."

"Winning would look even better." Dev hitches his shoulders and lets them drop. "Which we were definitely going to."

"Same here," Raven says morosely. "And at our competition you can audition for colleges, maybe even get a scholarship. Now none of that is going to happen for us."

"Well, we can't change the weather." Jermaine pats Raven's shoulder. "We'll just have to make the best of it."

He looks at the others. "The clerk said there's a common room with board games. Maybe we could all meet up there, pool our food, play a few games?"

And when Knox and the others agree, it's all I can do not to kiss Jermaine for his suggestion. Instead of sitting in our rooms watching TV, we will be hanging out with beautiful strangers.

One beautiful stranger in particular.

4

READY FOR THE NIGHT

Friday, 9:03 PM

AFTER WE ALL MAKE PLANS TO MEET UP IN THE COMMON ROOM IN half an hour, the robotics team heads to the front desk to get their rooms sorted out. My group sets out for the elevator, which I vaguely remember from Stuart's laminated map is at the very back of the motel. On the left, a sign reading COMMON ROOM/BREAKFAST and FITNESS ROOM points down a branching hallway. We keep going straight, following the main concourse, walking past empty meeting rooms full of tables set up for no one.

The space widens into a large carpeted area with a ceiling that's at least thirty feet tall. Ahead and to the left is the kind of swimming pool meant to appeal to children, with fake islands and a turquoise plastic tube slide. On the far side of the pool are two floors of rooms with sliding glass doors.

Looming directly ahead of us is some kind of tall hut, or maybe a tree house minus the tree. Two stories high and about forty feet across, it's circular, with a gray thatched roof and an open top floor surrounded by railings. The structure is painted purple, orange, and turquoise. The top story is bigger than the bottom, and the supports holding it up have been made to look like tigers with outstretched tails. A chain blocks across a stairway leading up to the darkened second floor. The patio area holds a half-dozen tables and is decorated with randomly spaced five-foot-tall wooden tiki heads.

"What in the heck is this thing?" Min's mouth falls open as she tilts her head back. "Is that roof made of palm fronds?"

I think she's right. They look both real and really old, to the point they're dusty. Where would you even get those around here?

"It's a tiki bar," Adam says. "It's called the Tiger's Tail."

"How do you know that?" Min asks.

"I looked up the motel on my phone when Mrs. McElroy was checking in," Adam says. "The Yelp review said, 'Come for the drinks, stay for the smell of chlorine.' But another reviewer said they had really good mai tais."

"In my church, we don't believe in drinking," Jermaine says.

"But what if drinking believes in you?" Min says, already cracking herself up.

Jermaine shrugs, unperturbed. "I don't even know exactly what a tiki bar or a mai tai is."

"Probably the people who come here don't know what those things are, either," Raven says. "I mean, I've been to Hawaii three times, but how many other people can say that? We're in the middle of the United States. Not exactly a tropical paradise."

"Whatever mai tais are, no one's drinking them tonight," Adam says.

"I guess it's not the kind of spot you want to head to during a blizzard," I say.

"Where did the clerk say that elevator was again?" Min sighs. "I feel like I've been dragging my suitcase for miles."

Adam points. "I think it's just past the swimming pool."

We turn left, walking with the rooms on our right and the pool on our left. There's even a little footbridge over it, complete with a NO DIVING sign. You'd have to have a lot of mai tais to think that was a good idea. The depth isn't even marked. I packed a swimming suit for our original hotel, which had a hot tub, but there's no sign of one here.

Finally, a normal hall with a regular-height ceiling opens up on our right, and we walk down it. When it turns left, we do, too. What seems like hundreds of yards later, we spot the elevator alcove. Min presses the button. When it comes, there's barely room for all of us plus our suitcases.

We spill into the corridor when the doors open again. Chocolate-brown wainscoting reaches waist high, and the wall above it is painted creamy beige. The carpet is patterned in various shades of brown that swoop and mingle together down the long, dimly lit corridor. The muddy colors mean it's impossible to tell if it's freshly vacuumed, caked with dirt, or something in between.

The corridor stretches endlessly in both directions. I look one way, then the other. They seem identical. Why didn't I pay attention to the map?

"Huh," Jermaine says as he turns his head back and forth. "Usually there would be a sign with arrows pointing which way to go depending on your room number."

I look at my key. I still can't get over that it's a real metal key, not a card. The attached diamond-shaped metal fob has the number. "We're in four twenty-three." I remember Stuart saying the rooms that had been added on to the second floor began with the number four.

"And we're in four fifty-two," Adam says. The nearest door says 222. "Now we just go to the next door," he says, "see what number it is, and then we'll know which direction to go."

Min checks the next door. "No, we won't. This is room two twenty-four, but we don't know where they put that new wing. Maybe it's at the beginning, or maybe it's at the end of all these numbers. Maybe it's even in the middle."

Grumbling, tired, and hungry, we pull our suitcases

down the shadowy corridor, turning when it meets up with another one. But the numbers here still start with two. No fours. There continue to be no signs on the wall at all, just the numbers on the doors. As we turn at the end of every corridor, turning and turning and turning but somehow never finding our block of rooms, the group splinters. I try to keep Min in sight. Even though her legs are shorter than mine, she's faster.

"Hey!" Min suddenly shouts. "These rooms start with four!"

"Really?" I turn to look for the others, but the hall behind me is empty.

After we locate our rooms and I twist the key in the door, I fumble for the light. The room is just as dreary and impersonal as I guessed it would be. I flop backward on the bed closest to the door. "Oh my God, I thought we would never find it." My nose tickles, and I sneeze. I turn my head toward the brown polyester comforter and sniff. "Ugh. It reeks of dust."

"No wonder! This whole place is like a time-warp mausoleum." Min darts in and out of the bathroom, then starts opening drawers in the bureau that holds the old boxy TV.

"What are you looking for?"

"A coffee maker. But there isn't one."

Sitting up, I scan the room. "No microwave, either. Which means this ravioli isn't going to do me much good."

After unwrapping the fruit pie, I wolf it down in about five bites.

"There's probably a microwave in the common room." In the summers, Min's family travels a lot, so she has more familiarity with how hotel rooms work. I haven't told her, but I was even excited about getting to stay at a Marriott tonight.

"Why do you want coffee now anyway?" I ask. "It's late."

"Might as well have fun, which means staying up even later." She puts her hands on her hips. "What, are you planning to go to bed at nine thirty? I mean, I may have implied to my mom that's what we were going to do, but that's boring."

"You're right." I'm tired of being the good girl. Of being the mom.

"Besides, don't you want to go hang out with that Knox, as in 'school of'?" She does a decent imitation of Maeve. "It looked like you were hoping he would volunteer to teach you a thing or two."

"Oh, shut up." Grabbing a pillow, I swing it at her.

"Ow! Stop it!" Min's half laughing and half-serious. "That hurts!"

"It's just a pillow!" Still, I stop.

Outside the window, which is covered by closed white curtains, the wind howls. Paintings—or rather, prints of paintings—hang on either side. The one closest to me is of two white vases filled with blobs of brick-red flowers. A few green lines suggest leaves. In front of the vases is another blob that might be a lemon. But that's not what makes me start to laugh.

"What's so funny?" Min asks.

I point, still laughing. "Look at that painting."

Min tilts her head. "It's like watercolor meets abstract done by a nine-year-old." She looks over her shoulder at me. "But I don't see why it's so funny."

For an answer, I point at the other painting. It's identical. It's the exact same print.

Her head swivels back and forth as she looks at the painting and its doppelgänger. "But why?"

"Maybe they got a deal."

"This whole place is weird. And I definitely don't want to spend one more second in this room than I have to. I just need to fix my hair before we go downstairs. You messed it up." Min flounces back into the bathroom. Her hair always looks tousled, but on-purpose tousled.

After hoisting my suitcase on the bed, I pull out the bag of mandarins and the bag of candy miniatures. Rooting around in my makeup bag, I find my reddest lipstick. In the bathroom, Min scooches over to make room for me.

"Do you think I should change my top?" She takes the lipstick from my hand and applies it to her mouth first, making a perfect Cupid's bow that I can give only to other people, never to myself.

Instead of answering, I say, "I saw you looking at that Valeria."

"She *is* on the robotics team. I like a girl who's good with her hands."

"TMI!" I snatch the lipstick back.

Five minutes later, we've both changed into black pants, part of the all-black outfits we were supposed to wear to the competition. Black provides a blank slate that doesn't distract from the character whose skin you're slipping into. Hers are sleek ponte and mine are Taclite pants, the favorite of backstage folks everywhere because of their million pockets.

Min's also wearing a white blouse that ties at the neck with a long, narrow black bow. It's innocent-looking, but combined with her red pout, it's also sexy. I put on a red sweater my moms got me for Christmas. The V-neck shows off my necklace. The sweater is made of cashmere, so soft I want to pet it.

We leave the room, convinced we're ready for the night to begin.

IS IT REALLY A COMPETITION?
Friday, 9:36 PM

FINDING THE ELEVATOR AGAIN IS NEARLY AS HARD AS FINDING our room was. As Min and I wander down one empty corridor and then another, I try to make a mental map. We turn left, then right, then left, then—wait, aren't we back where we started? Only the numbers here begin with two, not four. Then suddenly when we turn a corner, in a hall I feel we've already walked down a half-dozen times, there it is. The elevator.

While we're waiting, Min starts to laugh. She points, and I finally get it. A painting hangs on either side of the elevator. Identical to the ones in our room.

The door opens. After I press the button, Min looks up. "There's a mirror on the ceiling."

I tilt my head back, and we regard each other in the age-spotted silver. Her dark hair, my blond, our matching red lips. Her hands are empty, while mine hold the chocolates and mandarins. I forgot the tiny container of ravioli back in the room. Between regarding our mirrored selves and my body sensing the elevator's movement while my eyes insist I'm standing still, a wave of dizziness engulfs me. When the doors open, I stumble out into the knot of people a few feet away.

Just before I face-plant, a strong arm catches me. "Easy there, girl." Keeping his hand on my shoulder to steady me, Knox takes a step back and appraises me with a crooked grin. "Have you two been pregaming?"

Maeve raises one eyebrow. She's standing next to Jermaine, close enough that I'm glad Raven is not currently in view. "Ooh, Blondie's a lightweight!" Her tone is mocking.

"I like to think of it as being a cheap date." Knox winks at me.

"We weren't drinking!" I protest.

Min flashes me a look. I realize I sound like everything I don't want to be tonight: judgmental, boring, fading into the corner.

With a smirk, Valeria saves me from myself. " 'That's what she said.' "

"Come on," Knox says. "Let's go find that party room the clerk was talking about."

"You mean the common room?" Jermaine asks.

"Tonight it shall be known as the party room."

We reverse the course we took earlier, walking past the pool and turning right at the tiki bar. Min starts to sing "Drink with Me" from *Les Mis*, waggling her eyebrows when she sings about pretty girls.

"Wow!" Maeve says. "You've got an amazing voice."

Min abandons the song. "That's what I was supposed to sing in competition tomorrow." She sighs. "Part of me is still hoping the show can go on."

Maeve's full mouth twists. "Nothing's going to go on. I think we'll be stuck here all weekend."

Reality crashes over me. "I don't know how robotics competitions work, but we've been working toward ours for months." Going to state was a chance to perform in front of our peers, people who would appreciate just how hard we'd worked. How good we were. Not only that, but recruiters for college theater programs were going to be in the audience, checking out next year's seniors. Now we've had the rug pulled out from under us.

"Maybe people from the other side of the state made it in," Raven says as we walk into the lobby. Stuart is not at his desk. "I wonder if they're going on without us?"

Jealousy sinks its fangs into me. "Is it really a competition if half the people don't show?"

Jermaine shrugs. "It wouldn't be their fault. And you know how disappointed we would be if we made it all the way there and they said it was canceled or they weren't giving out prizes."

Knox turns down the hall. On the left are two sets of double doors, both standing open, that lead to the same large room. On the right are men's and women's restrooms and a tiny fitness center. Knox steps inside the big room, and his mouth falls open. "Wow!" He turns his head from side to side.

We crowd behind him. *Wow* is an understatement. It's not the furniture, which is mostly your basic cheap vinyl and metal tables and chairs. It's what's on the wood-paneled walls.

Every square inch is covered with old-timey knick-knacks, like a Cracker Barrel restaurant on steroids. I turn slowly, taking it all in. A cast-iron pan, leather ice skates, wooden skis, a rolling pin, a hoe, a battered red sled, an oil lantern, a wooden tennis racket, a hand-colored photograph of a lake, an orange sign for Keyser's general store, and what looks like a pair of pliers meant for a giant. Everything is faded, worn, dusty.

A long stainless-steel counter, which will presumably hold tomorrow's breakfast, runs along the right wall. At one end is a coffee carafe, but when Min puts a Styrofoam cup underneath and presses the pump hopefully, nothing comes out. Next to the coffee carafe is a vending machine. People are already feeding it quarters.

On the left side of the room, a worn blue couch and two matching recliners face an unlit fireplace. Next to it is a bookcase filled with faded board games and battered paperbacks. An old hunting rifle hangs over the fireplace, with a deer head above and more bric-a-brac on either side. On the mantelpiece is a framed photo of a woman with her hair piled on her head, two trophies, a woven picnic basket, a bowling pin, and a half-dozen clocks, all of them stopped.

"Those clocks are like this motel," a guy says behind me. It takes me a second to come up with his name. Dev. Under his thick brows, he has a thin, serious face. "Time has stopped here." He takes a pretzel from a half-empty bag, then holds the bag out to me.

"Thanks." I reach into his bag with my free hand. "And these are for everyone." I set my bags of oranges and miniature candy on the coffee table in front of the couch. I counted in our room. There's enough for everyone to have one orange and three pieces of candy—if I don't eat any candy.

"Thanks, Mom!" Raven says as she grabs at least five pieces of candy.

I shoot her a look, which bounces off her. I wish she wouldn't call me that in front of the others.

"Mom?" Dev echoes, glancing between us. We're the same age, and I'm white and Raven's Black. "Why is she calling you that?"

Before I can answer, Raven does. "Because Nell's a teen mom. She had her first baby at thirteen."

"First baby?" I repeat, bewildered.

She puts her arm around me. "Don't be modest, Nell." She turns to Dev. "She had her second six months ago. Not only is she managing to stay in school; she's the mainstay of our thespian troupe."

Dev is staring at me, his mouth half-open. Where he can't see it, Raven's pinching my upper arm. It's like improv, which I'm terrible at.

"Theater is just what I love to do," I say lamely, trying to play along. Even though it's the one true sentence I've told him, I'm not selling it. Hoping to avoid needing to lie again, I head to the back of the room, which is a long row of windows. They're as black as if someone painted over them. Behind me, Raven is talking about my imaginary kids. They're supposedly named Desiree and Frank, for reasons known only to her. Dev actually seems to be buying it. To hide my flushed face, I press it against a cold pane, cupping my hands around my eyes.

But what little I can see has been made featureless by the snow. Under the sides of my hands, the glass vibrates from the wind. I become newly aware of it howling outside. I've stopped noticing it because it never ceases, just changes slightly in pitch.

"Can you actually see anything out there?" Jermaine says from behind me.

I turn. "No. It's like we're in that short story about the evil little boy who has the power to make the rest of the world disappear."

His face lights up. "I saw that on *The Simpsons*."

"Yeah, that's where they got the idea," I say, looking past him. "First it was a short story in the fifties, and then it was a *Twilight Zone* episode." Out in the hall, Oscar is tipping back a small silver flask. "But it was a short story first." After several long swallows, Oscar finally caps the flask and slides it back in his pocket.

People have been adding to the pile of food on the coffee table. I walk over to check it out. Candy, chips, plus a few things that weren't in the motel store and must have come from suitcases or the vending machine. My mandarin oranges are the only healthy choice and also ignored. People seem to be going for anything they can immediately cram in their mouths. A giddiness is starting to fill the room. Voices are raised. Laughs are louder. Everyone seems to be flirting. Valeria appears, and Min makes a beeline for her, toying with the bow on her blouse.

When Adam shows up, he starts adding balls of newspaper to the fireplace and then stacking logs. The wind makes a weird hollow sound as it blows over the top of the chimney. When Adam lights the fire, it seems so tiny compared with the immensity of the storm. I start to shiver.

"Cold?" Knox appears at my side.

"This sweater isn't really warm enough. Maybe I should have worn my coat."

"And make us miss out on seeing how good it looks on you? Do you need help getting warm?" He drapes his arm around my shoulders. I shiver even more at his touch, although I try to hide it. Maybe tonight I can be the kind of cool girl someone like Knox would go for. A girl so used to compliments that she's almost bored by them.

Maeve, who was in the corner talking to Jermaine, struts up to us. Every eye is on her. Girls, guys, straight or gay—it doesn't matter. A sweatshirt is tied around her waist. She unties it and hands it to me.

"Cold? Put this on."

Knox takes his arm from around my shoulders, and I pull the sweatshirt over my head. It's plain and gray, so big I'm swimming in it. Next to Maeve, I feel myself fading away.

Knox raises his voice. "Hey, guys! Want to play a game?"

"Which one?" Adam leans down to look at the battered boxes in the bookcase.

"I've got a better idea than Clue or Life. How about Two Truths and a Lie? It should be easy for you guys. After all, you're actors."

6

A STORY WITHOUT WORDS
Friday, 9:57 PM

"Two Truths and a Lie?" Maeve claps her hands. "Ooh, I like this idea!"

"What are the rules again?" Dev asks as people begin to gather around Knox.

"You think of two truths and a lie about yourself and then tell them to the group. The truths should be something people don't already know about you. And then we vote on which one we think is a lie."

While Knox is speaking, Adam starts dragging over two dining room chairs. He puts them on the far side of one of the recliners. Other people follow suit, until there's a half circle around the fireplace, with the old blue couch in the middle. Knox sits on the center cushion, then pats the space next to him while looking at me. I glance behind me, but there's nobody there. Why did I do that? The kind of girl I want to be would just assume the gesture was meant for her.

Face flaming, I perch next to him. The couch is stained and faded, but suddenly it feels like the best seat in the house.

"And you can say them in any order, right?" Min asks, plopping down in one of the recliners. She grabs Valeria's hand and tugs. With a giggle the other girl sits next to her, hip to hip. They're so petite they can both fit.

Maeve gestures to Knox's other side. "Is this seat taken?" She shakes back her red hair.

"Not at all." Knox grins at her. Are they more than robotics team members to each other? But then again, I'm the one he asked to sit next to him. Not Maeve. *Me*. Doesn't that mean something?

"There's another version that I like even better," Oscar says, claiming the remaining recliner. "Everyone writes down their two truths and a lie and puts them in a hat. Then one person draws out a slip at random and reads it. The group has to vote on whether that person wrote it. Then the person who really wrote it reads it again, and this time the group votes on which one is the lie. You get a point for every time you guess right."

Adam says, "So basically we have to do a good job of

selling the lie." He's sitting on the end of our half circle, closest to the fire.

"Or acting," Knox says. "But yes, basically, you need to make us believe that all three things are equally plausible. Or even better, equally implausible."

In my head, I hear Mrs. McElroy's voice: *"As an actor, you don't have a tangible product to sell. You are your own product. And if you don't have confidence, you have nothing to sell."*

That's my problem. Even though I love acting, what I'm really good at is makeup, costumes, sets, and lighting. Once I'm onstage instead of backstage, any confidence deserts me. The whole time I'm saying my lines, a voice in the back of my head is busy commenting, tearing me down.

Yet all I've ever wanted to do since I was a little kid is act. Once I figured out that the people on TV weren't real-real, that they were characters portrayed by actors, it was like watching magic happen right in front of me. Somehow ordinary people were making me believe they were cruel murderers, brave soldiers, or desperate gamblers. I used to turn off the sound so I could figure out how their bodies made false seem true. How they moved their arms, their hands, even their feet. How they revealed their feelings by the way they raised their eyebrows or pressed their lips together. How even their tongues told a story without words, the tip poking out in a flash of displeasure or desire or sometimes even mockery. Standing in front of the

TV, I would mimic the actor's stances, gestures, and facial expressions.

"If we're going to do Oscar's version," Adam says, "we're going to need something to write with. I'll go ask Stuart if we can borrow some pens and scratch paper."

Jermaine says, "So it's thespians versus robot engineers in a game where the best liar wins. Do you guys really think you have a chance against the professionals?" Raven gives him a high five.

"You might be surprised," Oscar says. I wonder if I'm the only one who notices his words sliding into one another. Whatever is in his silver flask must be kicking in.

Adam comes back with a handful of pens, a square yellow pad, and Stuart.

"So you guys are going to play a game, huh?" Stuart gestures at the bookcase. "We've got Yahtzee, Clue, and Monopoly. I think there's even an old game of Twister in there."

"We're doing Two Truths and a Lie," Knox says. While Adam starts passing out pens and yellow paper slips torn from the *While You Were Out* pad, he explains to Stuart how the game works. I bend over my knees, shielding my paper with one hand, as he gives an example. "Like I might write down, 'I have met Tom Cruise. I have eighteen first cousins. I am color-blind.'"

Stuart tilts his head, revealing the bald spot beginning to peek through the hair on his crown. "And then everyone else has to guess which two are true?"

"Yes, but since we're putting all the slips together, first people have to guess who wrote those three."

Stuart nods. "So which is it? Which is the lie?"

Knox grins. "The one about cousins. I only have five." He points at Stuart. "Do you want to play?"

"Me?" Stuart takes a step back. "No thanks. I need to keep an eye on the front desk. In fact, I'll just go check to make sure no one needs me."

The whole time they've been talking, I've been debating what to write. What will make Knox regard me with interest? What are truths my team doesn't already know? And what's a lie people won't easily guess?

I look around. Some people are writing as fast as they can, while others tap their pens against their lips, staring up at the ceiling. Raven takes a Red Vine from the table and chews it thoughtfully.

I finally settle for: *I have been given a check for five thousand dollars. I have martial arts training. I once shaved my brother's leg while he was sleeping.* On my sixteenth birthday, my grandma gave me the money for my college fund. And my brother was dead asleep because he had been at a party. As for martial arts, I only wish it were true. I'd love to be a badass ninja instead of just myself.

When Knox finally starts to write, it takes him only a few seconds. "Okay, everybody, finish up," he says. "Now we just need a hat." But no one's wearing a hat, not even a beanie.

Stuart has reappeared. Presumably we are more interesting than standing at a desk waiting for guests that will never come. He takes the wicker picnic basket from the mantel. "How about this?" After opening the lid, he carries it from person to person so that we can toss our slips inside.

I let go of my folded paper, already wishing I had written something else. Something better. Something cooler.

7

EVERYONE DESERVES TO BE A CHARACTER

Friday, 10:12 PM

ONCE ALL THE SLIPS OF PAPER ARE IN THE BASKET, STUART STIRS them around with his free hand, then closes the lid. But Raven grabs the basket as he starts to hand it to Knox.

"I call first dibs to draw," she crows.

Min and I exchange a wordless look. Sometimes we joke that if Mrs. McElroy ever put on *Romeo and Juliet*, Raven would figure out a way to play both parts.

She raises the basket overhead and shakes it, stopping abruptly when a cloud of gray dust sifts down on her tight curls. Coughing, she sets it on her lap, then reaches under the lid. Her hand emerges with a folded slip.

"Read it out loud," Knox says.

"Okay." She uses an English accent, so cartoonish I half expect her to end each sentence with *guv'ner*. Almost every theater kid secretly thinks they're as good as Meryl Streep at accents. And nearly every one of them is wrong. " 'I'm not ticklish. I can impersonate any character on *The Simpsons*. I've never been French-kissed.' "

At that last one, something in the room changes. *French-kissed!* It's exciting. Edgy. People grin and make "ooh" noises.

"Never been French-kissed, huh?" Knox wiggles an eyebrow suggestively. "Do you guys think that sounds like Raven?"

For an answer, Raven leans toward Jermaine. She braces one hand on the edge of his seat and cups the back of his head with the other. And then she goes in for the kiss. At first Jermaine's eyes widen, but then they close. The rest of the room cheers and stamps their feet. When they finally finish, Raven stands up and takes a bow.

As she sits back down, Knox says, "Okay, we know it's not either of them."

"Or that the kissing one was the lie," Adam points out.

"Unless it was the first kiss for one of them," Maeve says. "Or there weren't any tongues involved."

Raven winks. "No worries on that front." Jermaine sits silent, still looking a little stunned.

"Okay, so probably not Raven or Jermaine." Knox looks around. "Who do you guys think it is?"

"I vote for Nell." Raven offers me a smirk, and I feel a little bit betrayed.

"No, I'm sure it's Dev," Jermaine says.

"Hmm." Knox leans forward. "Let's think this through." He points. "Jermaine and Raven are already out." He continues his way around the half circle. "I very much doubt it could be Valeria. Or Min, for that matter." He looks over at me. "Could it be Nell?"

I toss my hair and pucker my lips, trying to look sexy. But Maeve's oversize gray sweatshirt does me no favors.

To my disappointment, Knox says, "Hmm, she does seem promising." He points at each person in turn. "I've seen enough at our, um, practices, to know it's not Maeve. Maybe Dev?" Dev tries to pull off a smile, but it doesn't succeed. "Or Adam?" Adam shrugs, but I'm pretty sure he's only pretending not to care.

A bell sounds out in the hall. Stuart straightens up. "Sounds like we have another refugee," he says.

When we vote, it's six for me and four for Dev. I vote for him, but Raven and even Adam raise their hands for me. And they're on my team! Do people really think I'm so bland and boring that I've never been kissed? Or—and this cheers me up—maybe they know that sentence is definitely the lie.

Besides, I have been French-kissed. Once in seventh grade.

While I'm thinking, Dev points to his chest. "Actually, it's me."

Sotto voce, Knox says to me, "Well, that's a relief."

Oscar jumps to his feet, staggering a little. "I think we need to test out which is the truth and which the lie. Let's see if the tickling one is true!" He grins as he wiggles his fingers in the air.

"Go for it!" Maeve shouts, while others offer encouragement.

Oscar approaches Dev with fingers outstretched. Dev makes no move to protect himself, leaving his palms cupped over his knees. As Oscar starts tickling his ribs, he doesn't squirm away. He just stares straight ahead, trying, and mostly succeeding, to look neutral, even bored.

But then Oscar ducks his head and drops a kiss on Dev. Right on the lips. It only lasts for a second or two, but it's long enough that Dev jerks his head back, eyes wide. And now people are shouting approval even louder than they did for Raven.

"Fixed it for you, dude." Oscar sits back down.

I can't believe Oscar just did that. It's incredibly stupid. If Mrs. McElroy were here, she would already be on the phone to child protective services, no matter that Dev didn't really seem to mind. Even if he's over eighteen, which is possible, the school district would still have a lot to say. At a minimum, Oscar would be out of his student teacher job.

As for Dev, he just draws the back of his hand across his lips, but not as if he's thinking about wiping off Oscar's germs. Instead he looks thoughtful. Like he's considering what just happened and whether he liked it.

Maeve jumps to her feet. "Oh, no you don't, Oscar. You can't recruit Dev to your team without letting him scope out the competition."

Dev's eyes go wide as he drops his hand. He opens his mouth—I'm pretty sure it's to say the word *no*—but before he can say anything, Maeve is on him like a lamprey eel. Her kiss is as fierce as a bite. She's holding on to Dev's ears like handles as he twists under her onslaught. And when she triumphantly lifts her head, she's literally left her mark on him—a smeared blur of red lipstick that's not just on his lips but halfway up to his nose and down his chin.

Maeve saunters back to her seat, but not before snatching up a handful of Doritos from the coffee table. Knox gives her a high five after she sits down.

"So can you really do any character on *The Simpsons*?" Adam asks, trying to help steer our ship into calmer waters. And when Dev nods, he says, "Do Bart!"

"Eat my shorts!" He captures Bart's brattiness perfectly.

"Do Homer!" Jermaine demands.

"Mmm, doughnuts," Dev says, followed by, "Why, you little...!"

Valeria is grinning. "How about Maggie?"

He raises one eyebrow. "You do know that Maggie basically just sucks her pacifier, and the most well-known time she spoke, it was voiced by Liz Taylor?" When she shrugs, he says, "Daddy!" in a high, soft voice.

"Do Apu!" a man says from the edge of the room. We all turn. We were so engrossed in our game that we hadn't noticed him. He's tall and spindly, with red hair. In one hand, he's got a roller suitcase with a smaller bag strapped on top, and in the other he has one of those little microwavable cups. "That should be a natural!"

The smile falls from Dev's face like a plate from a shelf. The whole room goes silent.

"Sorry to interrupt your game, guys." The man walks over to the microwave and sticks in the cup. He hits a couple of buttons, and it begins to hum. "Just let me heat up my dinner, and then I'll leave you in peace."

"So you think just because my parents are from India that I should be a fan of Apu?" Dev says. "I hate him. Kids on the playground would always come up to me and mimic that accent. Do you know how many times I heard 'Thank you, come again!' or 'Hello, Mr. Homer!'?" His mimicry is as perfect as the others, but there's no life in it. He grimaces. "Of course the writers gave him an arranged marriage. And eight kids, which is basically a joke about India being overpopulated. Even working in the Kwik-E-Mart was a stereotype."

"It's not a stereotype if it's true," the man says stubbornly.

Dev takes a deep breath and closes his eyes for a second

before he continues. "Just because he's not a bloodthirsty terrorist or some crazy religious martyr doesn't mean it's not hurtful. Just because he's nice, even lovable, doesn't make it okay. Apu never changes. He doesn't get to grow like the other characters. Even Flanders became a widower. Everyone deserves to be a character, not a caricature."

"Well, excuse me for having an opinion." The microwave bings, and the man takes out his ravioli.

The room is totally silent as we watch him leave.

STARING DAGGERS
Friday, 10:24 PM

"WOW!" AS SOON AS THE GUY LEAVES, JERMAINE RAISES HIS EYE-brows and blinks rapidly, miming shock. "What a jerk!"

People chime in to agree, only with more colorful words.

After a minute, Knox cuts his hand through the air. "Okay, let's stop letting that guy spoil our night. He's gone, and we should just forget about him." He turns to Valeria. "It's your turn to draw."

Reaching in the basket, she starts to take out a slip. But then she shakes her head, black curls tumbling over her face. "That one didn't feel right." She grabs another and gets to her feet. She puts on a southern accent, turning every *I* to *ah*. It's slightly more credible than Raven's English one.

"Okay, it says, 'I still laugh when the ketchup makes that farting sound. I'm addicted to sniffing cologne. I never learned how to swim.'"

"First we need to vote on whether Valeria wrote it," Knox says.

"Cologne is named after Cologne, Germany," Dev says. "The city. The guy who invented it had just moved there from Italy."

Knox makes a scoffing noise. "Jeez, are you trying to sound like someone who spends their evenings watching *Jeopardy!* reruns? That whole kissing thing is going to be a one-off if you're not careful."

"I don't think any of us girls wrote it," Min says. "Girls wear perfume, and guys wear cologne."

Min's right, I think, grabbing a mandarin. It does sound like a guy. Dev's already had his turn, so that leaves—I look around the half circle as I sink my fingernails in the skin and peel it back—Adam, Oscar, Knox, and Jermaine. And when my eyes land on Jermaine, I suddenly just know. Ketchup farts—he does like that simple, juvenile humor. Earlier in the van, he was making jokes after the air suddenly turned pungent and everyone denied being the source. The others also guess Jermaine as the source.

I point at him. "My vote goes for Jermaine."

Maeve purses her lips. "And I'm voting for Adam."

Knox and Adam each get one vote. The rest of us choose Jermaine.

"You're right." He stands up. When Valeria offers him the slip of paper, he waves it away. He puts on a French accent that he can barely control. It mostly involves adding a lot of extra *thes*—pronounced *zee*—and turning short *I* sounds into long *E* sounds.

"Ouch." Wincing, Dev puts his hands over his ears as Jermaine reads the three sentences.

"Don't quit your day job!" Adam says with a grin.

Jermaine looks genuinely hurt. "I didn't think it was that bad."

"Okay, okay," Knox says. "Let's go around and say which one we think is the lie." He turns to me with those piercing blue eyes.

"Sniffing cologne," I say. "I don't see how you could really be addicted to that." After I'm done talking, I keep looking at Knox. In fact, I lean closer. Something about knowing we'll never see each other again makes me braver. Less self-conscious despite the shapeless gray sweatshirt I'm wearing.

With his index finger, Knox traces the fine gold chain across the nape of my neck. I can sense more than see Maeve staring daggers at me.

Most of the others choose swimming as the lie. Valeria, Min, and Dev join me in choosing cologne.

"And the answer is..." Knox looks at Jermaine.

This time Jermaine abandons his accent. "The cologne one was the lie."

Knox removes his finger, and I try not to feel bereft.

"Why don't you know how to swim?" Oscar asks. Unlike most of us, Jermaine looks and moves like the athlete he is.

He shrugs. "Swimming's for rich kids. It's like a country-club sport. In my neighborhood, there's no public pool, and even if there was, my folks wouldn't have had the money for lessons."

I think back to my moms taking turns teaching me, back when we lived in Los Angeles. "Couldn't they have taught you how to swim?"

He lifts his chin. "Not when they don't know how to themselves. The few times we've been, my mama will lie out next to a pool, but I've never seen her in the water. I used to try to get her to come in, but she was always worried about what the chlorine would do to her hair."

"That's too bad," I say, remembering gliding through the cool liquid, the soft shushing sound as it lapped against the sides of the pool. "I love swimming. It's so peaceful."

"You LA girls probably swim before you can walk,"

Adam says, "but around here a pool doesn't make as much sense, not when you can't use it for months on end."

"You're from LA, huh?" Knox looks at me with interest. "I should have guessed."

Feeling myself expand under his gaze, I duck my head and tuck a strand of hair behind my ear. I'm conscious of being the only blond in the room.

"But you were in the pool at that party at Becca's last summer," Min is saying to Jermaine.

"It's not like people go to those parties to swim laps," Jermaine says. "I just splash around in the shallow end."

Maeve has been rifling through the remains of the food on the coffee table. Now she picks up a bag of chips, shakes the last crumbs onto her outstretched palm, and then licks them off.

Out of the corner of my eye, I see Knox watching her out of the corner of *his* eye. With every swipe of her pink tongue, I feel myself diminishing.

I force myself to look away just as Linus, the guy Knox's group picked up, walks into the room. He's in his stocking feet and carrying an ice bucket.

He stops when he sees us, looking surprised. "Oh, hey, folks. I didn't expect to see y'all again." His southern accent is the real thing. His eyes go from face to face. "Hold up; looks like you made some new friends."

"There's actually another group of students that got stranded here," Knox explains. "Everybody, this is Linus. We helped him after his car slid off the road."

People nod, say hello, or offer him a small wave.

"I'm much obliged to you for picking me up. That is one big ole storm. Without y'all, I could've frozen to death."

He's not exaggerating. I'm still not used to Midwest temperatures. It's not unheard-of for it to get below zero degrees, which just seems wrong. It's called zero for a reason.

"So what'cha y'all doing?" Linus says, taking in the snacks, the picnic basket, the half circle around the fire.

"Playing a game," Raven volunteers.

"Charades?"

"Two Truths and a Lie," Valeria says.

Linus walks over to the ice machine and opens the little metal door. "I'll just get my ice and let y'all get back to it."

After he leaves, a sudden gust of wind blows through the room, making the fire gutter.

"Where did that come from?" Maeve wraps her arms around herself, shivering. And of course Knox puts his arm around her. I just wish she hadn't given me her stupid huge sweatshirt. But the room does feel suddenly colder, the outside closer.

"Who knows?" I say. "This place feels like it's falling

apart. It's clear no one has really stayed here for years. Maybe even decades."

Then I see something that makes all my blood rush to my face, makes me forget the cold. Because Stuart is back in the corner of the common room, glaring at me.

"Sorry," I say weakly. "I didn't see you there."

FOR YOU TO FIND OUT

Friday, 10:31 PM

"Uhh, umm," I stammer, wishing I could just disappear. "I'm so sorry. I didn't mean it. I was just—talking."

"Don't worry about it." Stuart bites off the words. He closes his eyes and takes a deep breath before continuing. "It's not news this place needs work. The local area's been hollowing out for decades. Just little towns, the kind that people move away from. After I left, the box factory closed down. My folks had a hard time keeping up. They tried the conference-center idea, but that didn't really work out. Then a Hampton Inn opened up thirty miles down the road." He sniffs. "That was the last straw. It turned into a death spiral. My folks didn't have the money to maintain things, and the less maintained this place was, the fewer guests stayed here, meaning even less money to fix things up. The Yelp reviews were cruel."

I exchange a glance with Adam. I know we're both remembering what Yelp said about the Tiger's Tail.

"My folks never complained, so I didn't know how bad it was, but basically they worked themselves to death. Mom died two weeks after Dad." The room is quiet except for the wind outside and the faint crackle of the fire. "After they were gone, I inherited everything. I sold my truck and came home. I've been trying to save this place, knowing how much it meant to them, but it's hard. In fact, it's pretty much impossible. Other than some high school girls in the summer, it's just me and Travis." He sees our blank looks. "The handyman. My parents took him in years ago. He's a little odd—he was in a car accident as a kid—but he's a hard worker."

Adam leans forward. "When we leave, I promise we'll post great reviews. About how this place has the kind of charm you can't get at a cookie-cutter chain." He gestures at the walls. "I mean, look at those decorations. You're not going to find that in a Hampton Inn."

"I appreciate the thought," Stuart says. "But I don't think it will make any difference." He pinches his lips between finger and thumb, then releases them. "I should let you guys get back to your game."

After he leaves, there is nothing but silence. Shame makes my shoulders hunch. Then Knox drapes his arm around them. "You just said what everyone else was thinking."

"Shh!" I put my finger to my lips. "I really don't want him to overhear anything else."

Knox gives my shoulder a squeeze, then takes his arm away. "Okay, Min, isn't it your turn to draw?"

Valeria passes the picnic basket to Min. She draws out a slip and gets to her feet. In a fake German accent not much better than Jermaine's French one, Min says, " 'I can fit twenty-one marshmallows in my mouth at once. I have seen a ghost. I have a crush on someone in this room.' "

The mood shifts again at the word *crush*. No one wants to keep thinking about Stuart's depressing situation, and now Min has given us a good excuse not to. Instead, we eye one another, grinning. Who's the crusher and who's the crushee?

"That's another one that's got to be from a guy!" Raven shakes her head. "No girl's dumb enough to spend her time counting how many marshmallows fit in her mouth."

"First of all, that's the one that could be the lie," Dev says. "And second of all, if a girl was bored she might do it. Plus maybe someone's just trying to fool us by picking things that sound like only a guy would do them. So that's another reason it could be a girl."

If it is a guy, I don't think it's Oscar. Even though he's

happy hanging out with teenagers, he still seems too much of a grown-up to stuff marshmallows in his mouth.

What about Adam? But he seems too serious for the marshmallow thing, and too down-to-earth to claim he's seen a ghost.

Could it be Knox? But if it's him, then who is his crush? I go still inside. Is it me?

Knox interrupts my thoughts. "Either way, it sounds like someone might have a talented mouth."

"Ooh, gross!" Maeve gives him a fake shove. He responds with a tickle. In seconds, they're play wrestling, leaving me wishing the sofa would just swallow me. Finally she pushes him away, and they both straighten up, smirking. So much for thinking I'm tops on Knox's list.

"Why don't we vote?" Dev says.

Min and Adam each get a vote, but everyone else votes for Knox. Including me.

Grinning, he throws his hands in the air. "You caught me! Now you have to choose which is the lie."

"The crush one," I say, even though it's the one I secretly hope is true. But I don't want it to be so obvious.

"The one about the ghost," Min says. One after another, we all vote on which statement is a lie. It's about half for crush, and half for ghost. No one picks marshmallows.

"Ha! Psyched you out!" Knox says. "The marshmallow one was the lie, because it wasn't twenty-one marshmallows. It was nineteen."

Oscar crosses his arms. "Basically you're saying that none of your statements was really a lie."

Knox shrugs. "We never said how much of a lie it had to be."

Dev makes a face. "It might not be against the letter of the rules, but it certainly seems against the spirit."

Adam rolls his shoulders. "Actors know there's plenty of room between truths and lies. And that there's ways to tell truths so they sound like lies and lies so they sound like truths."

"Yeah, yeah." Jermaine waves his hand. "But, Knox, you're kind of leaving us hanging here. You haven't answered the most important question of all." He leans forward. "Are we talking mini marshmallows or the regular-sized ones?"

"Regular."

Valeria wrinkles her nose. "How did you ever get that many marshmallows in your mouth anyway? And why?"

Knox shrugs. "It was a bet. And they cram together pretty good, and then the ones on the outside start to melt because of your saliva, which creates more room."

Just the thought of it makes my stomach turn.

"That sounds nasty!" Raven's lip curls.

"Did you swallow them?" Min asks with the kind of disgusted fascination with which you'd regard a boa constrictor ingesting a rabbit whole.

Clearly enjoying the attention, Knox grins. "I was afraid I'd choke. I just spit them in the sink."

"So what about the ghost?" I skirt the question I really want the answer to.

Leaning back, Knox laces his hands behind his head. "My family was in Alabama, staying at this old fancy house turned bed-and-breakfast. In the middle of the night, I woke up hungry. I went out to the dining room, because the hosts had left a snack basket on the table. But there was a guy already sitting there. I thought he was another guest, but when I got closer I saw he was dressed like a soldier from a long time ago. He had on this gray coat with little buttons all down the front and a cap with a short brim. When I asked him who he was, he just sighed. And then he disappeared." Knox lifts his hands and spreads his fingers. "Poof!"

"Weren't you scared?" Min asks, serious for once.

"I was only eight and half-asleep. I just grabbed a granola bar and went to bed. The next day I told the hosts. They said that during the Civil War, a Confederate soldier and his mother had been visiting. Then a Union soldier spotted him and shot him. Right where I saw him. The lady said his ghost only walks around or sometimes sits down. He never talks to anyone, never answers anyone. She did say that he liked to tilt picture frames. She was always having to straighten them."

As a shiver dances over my skin, something falls from the mantel, landing with a crash as loud as a thunderbolt.

We all scream. I clutch Knox, but Maeve does, too.

I finally find my voice. "What happened?"

Jermaine gets up and picks the object off the floor. It's the photo that was on mantel. He turns it toward us. Now the woman with her hair piled on her head is nearly obscured by the crazed glass.

As we stare at it, a middle-aged man wearing a button-down gray shirt and a dark flat cap enters the common room. Remembering Knox's ghost, I gasp, and Valeria lets out a little shriek.

"Oh, um, sorry." He holds up the book he's carrying, his finger marking a place. "I thought I'd come down and read in front of the fire. I didn't expect there to be any other guests tonight. Not with the way it is outside."

Adam answers. "Our two teams were going to competitions, but the blizzard stranded us both here."

He brightens. "Oh, really? What sport do you guys play? I listen to a lot of games on my radio when I'm driving. I'm a trucker."

"It's not really sports," Knox says. "Half of us are on a robotics team, and half of us are actors."

"Oh." He smiles, but it's clear the answer doesn't interest him. "That's uh—nice. My name's Brian, by the way. I'll just leave you to . . . whatever it is you were doing." He gives us a shy smile and goes back down the hall.

As soon as he does, Valeria says, "Don't think you're

getting off the hook, Knox. You still haven't answered the most important question. Who do you have a crush on?"

Dev leans forward. "Yeah, tell us the truth, the whole truth, and nothing but the truth, so help you God?"

I hold my breath as he looks around the half circle.

"You already know which statements are true." Knox's crooked grin cracks my heart wide open.

"But it's not the whole truth," Min says. "You didn't say who the crush was."

"It's Nell, isn't it?" Raven tips me a wink.

At the sound of my name, a pulse of heat runs from my heels to the top of my head, while Maeve makes a scoffing noise.

"I think it's Maeve," Valeria says. Min shoots her a look.

Knox puts his arms around both of us, pulling us in tight so that Maeve's and my faces are only inches from each other. Her lips pull back, baring her teeth. This close to Maeve, her made-up face is just a smear of colors. She smells of sweat and perfume.

"That's for me to know," Knox says, squeezing and then releasing us. "And for you to find out."

10

I LIKE TO WATCH PEOPLE DIE

Friday, 10:47 PM

MIN HANDS THE BASKET TO ME. "YOUR TURN."

I stir my hand in the rustling folded papers. Then—
"Ouch!" I pull back my empty hand and shake out my
fingers.

"What's the matter?" Min leans toward me.

I try to examine my fingertips in the dim light. "I must
have gotten a paper cut." But I don't see a single scratch or
bead of blood.

It felt like something bit me. Or shocked me. Or was it
more like a burn? Already the details are fading. I stir the
papers while looking in vain for a spider or a splinter of
wicker, some explanation.

"Don't look!" Valeria shakes a finger. "No cheating."

I flip the lid of the picnic basket down so that my hand disappears underneath it. Making a show of staring off to one side, I ruffle the papers again.

Again, I feel a sting in my fingertips. Instead of pulling back, I wrap my hand around the offending folded square and squeeze, crushing it. It feels like I just reached into a table lamp and crushed the light bulb inside: hot, then sharp, then electrical. I yank my clenched fist out of the picnic basket and drop the balled-up paper on my knee. It looks totally ordinary. It's not on fire or covered with broken glass. It's just a crumpled paper. Gingerly, I unfold and smooth it out.

But it's just a neon-yellow square with block printing on one side and *While You Were Out* printed on the other. Innocuous. It's silly that I imagined it hurt me.

And then I raise the slip of paper and actually take in the words written on it. As I read, an icy finger traces its way down my spine.

As everyone waits for me to read it aloud, the only sounds are the wind howling outside and the fire crackling inside. I start when Dev begins noisily crunching through the last of his pretzels.

Despite being written in all caps, the bulleted list doesn't seem like a shout. Instead, it feels like a whisper. Like a razor-sharp knife slipping between your ribs so fast you don't even feel pain until it's too late.

I make a noise halfway between a hum and a groan. "I don't know about this one, guys. Maybe I should pick another one."

"Come on!" Jermaine slaps his thighs for emphasis. "Just read what it says!"

"Let me see it." Knox tries to take it from my hand. "Are you having trouble reading the handwriting?"

I pull it out of reach, ignoring the warm press of his body against mine. "That's not the issue."

"Are you stuck trying to think of a good accent?" Min says sympathetically. "It's okay. Just read it."

"She probably drew her own slip, and now she's trying to psych us out that it's not her," Maeve says with a smirk. "Either way, Blondie, just read it."

The chant is taken up around the circle. "Read it! Read it!" With each repetition, it increases in volume. People add claps and stomp their feet.

It stops only when I stand up. I clear my throat. "Okay, the first one is 'I like to watch people die.'"

Raven gasps and puts her hand over her mouth. At the same time, Dev snorts. I guess what he's thinking. That this one is so obviously the lie. Unless maybe there is some stupid twist, like they only wrote down half the sentence and the rest is *in scary movies*.

I move on. "The second one is 'My least-favorite food is mushrooms.'"

"You and everybody else," Knox mutters. "Slimy *and* rubbery."

I don't bother saying I love mushrooms. Instead I read out the last line.

"The third one is 'I've lost count of how many people I've killed.'"

11

ALL WE KNOW
Friday, 10:55 PM

KNOX FROWNS AND CROSSES HIS ARMS. "OKAY, WHO DIDN'T understand the rules? It's supposed to be two truths and a lie, not two lies and a truth."

We eye one another, but no one volunteers it was them.

"Come on," he says impatiently. "Fess up. Who wrote it and didn't know what they were doing?"

"Wait," Oscar says. "So you think there are two lies? Because obviously, the thing about not liking mushrooms is true. Read the other two again, Nell."

" 'I like to watch people die.' " My voice shakes despite my attempt to control it. "And the other is, 'I've lost count of how many people I've killed.' "

"Okay." Dev's thick brows draw together. "I think we can all agree that the part about mushrooms is one of the true statements. So if nobody made a mistake and wrote down two lies, what does that mean? That someone in this room is a serial killer?"

Raven clutches Jermaine. "A serial killer! That's so scary!" He puts his arm around her, and she rests her cheek against his broad chest.

I try to corral my thoughts. I know my team members almost as well as I know myself, inside and out. Since I help with quick costume changes backstage, I know their bodies nearly as well as my own. And as unofficial team mom, I know their minds and hearts. Not only is no one on my team capable of killing anyone, but they're also not capable of telling such awful lies for fun.

So it has to be someone on the other team. And since Dev and Knox have already played, that leaves Maeve, Valeria, and Oscar.

Meanwhile, the robotics team is looking at our theater troupe with the same suspicious, creeped-out look my team is wearing. Only they're side-eyeing everyone but Jermaine.

They're even looking at me.

I'm suddenly aware of how little we know about them. All we know about one another is what we've said in this room. And how much of that was even true? I mean, Dev might still think I'm the mother of two.

Maeve wrinkles her nose. "I don't know. If you were a serial killer, why would you announce it?"

Adam's voice is flat. "The only way anyone would admit they were a serial killer was if they were planning on killing everyone who heard it."

This all feels eerily familiar. And then I know why. "This is getting to be like a bad movie or book," I say. "A group of strangers, trapped at night in a creepy old motel during a blizzard. And then you add a killer, picking them off one by one."

"Stop!" Valeria squeals, and slaps her hands over her ears. Min shoots me a look as she puts her arm around her.

"None of this makes sense. It's got to be a joke, right?" Raven's voice rises at the end. It's clearly more wish than question.

"You're right," Oscar says. "Someone's just messing with us. Only it's not funny."

"Well, it's *kind of* a little bit funny," Knox says. "Making the girls scared and everything."

"If it is a joke, it's a pretty sick one," Adam says.

"But it's an obvious one," Jermaine says. "They obviously didn't want us to take it seriously. This long day and no real food is making us gullible. And whoever wrote it was clearly not thinking straight. So whoever it was, just admit it."

"Yeah, enough is enough," Adam says. "Fess up."

But no one says anything. Instead our gazes just bounce off one another.

Oscar presses his lips together. "Whoever did this is not going to admit it, not when everyone is this upset."

"Well, they can't keep it secret forever," Dev says. "And I still can't see why anyone would write that."

"Someone who was just looking for attention," Oscar says.

"It would have to be one of those people who thinks any attention is good attention," I say.

Maeve folds her arms. "Aren't actors supposed to be like that?"

As I try to find the words to refute her, Knox says, "Okay, it's easy enough to figure out. We'll just dump out the rest of the slips and everyone will claim theirs. And whoever doesn't have a slip, then that's the person who wrote it." He looks around. "So before we go through all that, why don't you just save yourself the awkwardness and admit it?"

He waits. But he's met with nothing but silence.

Picking up the basket, I upend it on the coffee table, amid the empty chip bags, discarded candy packages, and orange peels. I open three notes before I find my own. I put it on the other knee, not wanting it to even touch the scary one.

But when I look around the half circle, there are no empty hands. Everyone is clutching a slip.

"So there's an extra slip," Adam says. "Someone must have put in two. Good effing joke."

"Does anyone recognize this handwriting?" I hand it to Valeria. She looks at it and shakes her head. After she passes it on, she rubs her fingers on her pant leg.

I lean closer. "Did you feel it, too? Like it kind of hurt to touch it?"

She acts like she doesn't know what I'm talking about. "What? It's just a piece of paper."

"The writing is in all caps." Raven looks closer. "My dad writes like that."

"I think it's a guy," Valeria says softly. "Girls usually have prettier handwriting."

It makes its way back to me, even though I most definitely don't want it. I set it back on my knee. "The letters are so blocky and square. I think whoever wrote it was trying to disguise their own writing."

"Face it. Whoever it is"—Adam waves his hand—"they're never going to say."

"I don't think I want to play this game anymore." Valeria's eyes are huge.

Maeve frowns. "But there's no point in going to bed, not when we've been having fun."

"Is that what we've been having?" Dev asks softly. "I feel like there's something really wrong with this place. Like it doesn't want us here."

As he is speaking, the wind picks up with a huge moan.

A sudden gust blows straight down the chimney, making the fire gutter again. Raven screams and Valeria joins in. Min puts her arms around her.

Out in the hall, there's a series of soft, surreptitious sounds.

And then I see it. A hooded figure sneaking up on us. Something long and narrow rests on its shoulder.

It looks like a shotgun.

12

HISTORY'S REPEATING ITSELF
Friday, 11:08 PM

"Gun!" I shriek. "He's got a gun!" Blood roars in my ears as my vision goes blurry.

As people start to scream, Knox somersaults backward over the couch and disappears. My knees buckle when I get to my feet. Electric with terror, I raise my arms like they will somehow provide protection. My limbs feel slow and heavy. Around me, everyone is scrambling for cover, shrieking and shouting.

Even the guy with a gun. Yelling incoherently, he takes it off his shoulder. Holding it by the barrel, he starts slicing it through the air. As he steps in from the shadowed hallway, I blink, trying to square what I see now with what I saw a few seconds ago. I realize two things.

One, it's Travis, the handyman who mopped up the melting snow we tracked in. He's wearing a black sweatshirt with the hood pulled up.

And two, what he's holding actually isn't a rifle. It's a baseball bat. A bat he's now swinging wildly through the luckily empty air.

"Where is he?" he shouts. "Who's got the gun?" He's clearly ready to use the imaginary bad guy's skull for a home run. Adam starts creeping up behind him, his own fingers wrapped around the fireplace poker.

I shout out a swear followed by, "Hold up, everybody! It's okay! There's nobody. I was wrong. I thought that bat was a gun!"

Letting the bat fall to his side, Travis stares at me.

Things are just starting to calm down—people have stopped screaming (or at least screaming as much)—when I catch sight of a man in the hall moving from shadow to shadow. It's Stuart. And he really does have a gun. Both hands are wrapped around a handgun, his elbows pressed against his ribs. Gone is the genial guy who checked us in. In his place is a man who moves like an assassin, slipping forward in a crouch, his head on a swivel.

Terror turns my blood to slush. Stuart's looking for a nonexistent killer. And if the way everything else has gone tonight is any indication, he might just end up accidentally turning into a killer himself.

"Stuart!" I shout. "It's okay! There's no gun."

He doesn't answer, just steps into the room, running his eyes over the frightened faces staring at him from behind furniture. Meanwhile, Travis seems completely unaware that Adam is standing behind him, still holding the fireplace poker at the ready. But Stuart sees him and starts to swing the gun in Adam's direction.

"Everything's okay," I shout again, patting the air with empty hands when really I want to fist them in my hair and tear it out. Adam is going to get shot, and it will be my fault. "Nobody's going to hurt anyone! I made a mistake. I thought Travis's bat was a rifle!"

After a long second, Stuart drops the gun to his side. Feeling like a marionette that's just had its strings cut, I fall more than sit on the couch. Except for everyone's noisy breathing, the room grows quiet.

Min and Valeria peek in from the swinging door that must lead to the kitchen. Oscar slowly stands up from behind his recliner. On hands and knees, Maeve peeps around one corner of the couch, while Knox looks around the other. Dev unpeels himself from the wall next to the fireplace. Adam lets the poker drop to his side.

"What are you saying?" Travis swipes his long gray-ing blond hair back, bringing the dent in his head into sharper relief. "Travis heard the screaming. He thought something was wrong." His brows are drawn together in puzzlement.

"I was wrong," I repeat. "I'm sorry. I saw you in the shadows out in the hall and thought your bat was a gun."

Stuart slips his handgun into the back of his waistband as Raven steps out from behind the vending machine, where she and Jermaine had squeezed themselves.

"I thought we were all going to die!" She breaks into tears, and Jermaine takes her into his arms.

Out in the hall, the few guests we met earlier have gathered in an anxious knot. I'm just thankful that because of her sleeping pill Mrs. McElroy is not one of them. The trucker guy, Brian, cautiously steps inside. "What's going on, you guys? I heard all this shouting."

"I was sure someone was being murdered," Linus adds.

"It was just a misunderstanding." Knox gets to his feet. When he puts a steadying hand on my shoulder, I realize I've been swaying.

The red-haired guy who was baiting Dev earlier says, "I was seriously thinking about just getting in my car and going. Not even looking in here. Only I was afraid I would freeze to death out there."

Brian makes a sour face. "And we wouldn't want that, Edgar." It's clear they know each other—and that there's no love lost between them.

Edgar says, "I couldn't help but think that history was repeating itself."

As Jermaine repeats, "History?" Stuart begins to shake his head warningly.

Edgar doesn't take the hint. "Two people died here over twenty years ago."

"People die everywhere," Oscar says. "Even in a motel. Heart attack, stroke..."

"Not these two," Edgar says with relish. "They were murdered. Stabbed to death while they were lying in bed. There was blood everywhere. Splashed on the walls. The bed was soaked with it like a sponge."

"Edgar!" Stuart says.

Valeria puts her hand across her mouth. "Who did it?"

"That's the thing." Edgar's grin is flat. "They still don't know."

13

PLEAD FOR INFORMATION
Friday, 11:36 PM

STABBED TO DEATH WHILE THEY WERE LYING IN BED? THINKING of my bed in our room, I shiver. What would it be like to be in bed and see a knife plunging toward you? *Into* you? To have that be the last sight you ever saw?

"All right, Edgar, that's enough," Stuart says. "We don't need to scare the kids."

Edgar snorts. "The kids! They're the ones who scared us with their screaming and carrying on."

"I think we should all just go back to bed." Stuart looks at us meaningfully. "Or go to bed in the first place. Every one of our guests deserves a good night's sleep."

He looks from face to face until all of us kids plus Oscar

nod in agreement. As he does, the other guests mutter good night and leave the common room.

"And before you go back to your rooms," Stuart says, "please clean up the mess you've made. Travis shouldn't have to be the one doing it."

Travis has set the bat down on the coffee table and is now picking up candy wrappers and the slips of paper from our game.

While we're still agreeing and apologizing, Stuart turns on his heel and leaves.

I feel small and stupid. I'm the one who overreacted to Travis, and now he's cleaning up after us without complaint.

"Here, Travis, don't worry; we'll get it," Adam says as he picks up an empty Twizzlers wrapper. I start gathering orange peels. Min and Valeria are righting overturned tables and chairs.

"Travis likes things to be clean." He carries what he's gathered to the garbage can.

"Then you certainly have the right job," Jermaine says. "Hey, can I ask you something? Why did you come out with a bat, anyway?"

"Sometimes Travis has to have a little talk with a guest," Travis says. He's not making eye contact with anyone.

"Because they're loud?" Raven asks.

He shrugs. "Or they don't pay, or they're smoking

Mary Jane, or they have someone in their room who don't belong there. Sometimes people turn out not to be the best guests. Beggars can't be choosy."

Choosers, I think. Which I realize is a very mom thought.

Knox leans out into the hall to look. Satisfied all the other adults are gone, he turns around and says, "What was that Edgar guy talking about?"

"You really don't want to know." Travis presses his lips together so hard they turn white, like he's afraid someone might reach in and yank out the truth.

Maeve steps closer, but her tone is coaxing rather than confrontational. "I think actually we do."

"Tonight's already been a roller-coaster ride, dude," Jermaine says. "What's one more loop?"

"You can't just leave us hanging," Knox says. An odd look crosses his face, like he's just remembered something.

"How about this?" I suggest. "How about if the people who don't want to hear it just go up to bed now?"

"Listen to Mom," Jermaine says.

But no one leaves. Instead we all stare expectantly at Travis. Finally, he exhales noisily.

"It's like Edgar said. A little over twenty years ago, this lady and this guy got stabbed to death in their room. For months, that's all the news around here talked about." He sighs again. "Why do you think this whole place is almost empty?"

"Stuart told us it was because people keep moving out of the area and the box factory went out of business," Dev says.

Travis shrugs. "Well, maybe. But it all started with the murders. Hang on."

When he leaves, he takes his bat. A minute later, he returns carrying a green photo album. After he sits on the couch, I sit on one side and Knox sits on the other. Maeve, clearly not wanting to lose her place beside Knox, manages to squeeze herself into the corner next to him.

Travis's elbow presses into my ribs. This close, I can smell him. It's not an unpleasant smell. Dusty, dry, and faintly sweet.

The photo album rests on his knees. He opens it to the first page. Maybe it's what I really smelled. It's the kind my grandma has, sticky sheets covered with clear plastic.

The first page holds a yellowing black-and-white newspaper clipping of two photos. One is of a girl in three-quarters profile. It looks like a senior portrait. She has light hair that falls to her shoulders, eyes that gaze off to her left, and closed lips that turn up in a tight, cautious smile. The other photo is of a laughing guy who is at least ten years older. His open mouth displays white, even teeth. His short dark hair looks as thick as fur.

"She kind of looks like you, Blondie," Maeve says. Travis nods.

I study the photo more closely. Does she?

Travis starts to flip through pages, leaving barely enough time to read the headlines.

DOUBLE HOMICIDE AT LOCAL MOTEL

VICTIMS OF DOUBLE MURDER IDENTIFIED

AUTHORITIES PLEAD FOR INFORMATION

MOTHER WON'T REST IN SEEKING JUSTICE FOR DAUGHTER

And then two Polaroid photos on facing pages. I put my hand on the page to stop Travis from turning it.

The first was taken from a hall just outside a room. On the wooden door, which is half-open, is the number 238. The shot is straight into the room, so while the bottom edge of the bed is visible on the left-hand side of the frame, you can't see more of it than that. Directly in front of the door is a bureau, seen from the side. On top is a TV, with a lamp on the far side. Between the bureau and the bed, a yellow blanket is puddled on the flat green carpet. Next to it is what looks like a gray shirt. In the back of the room, between the end of the bed and the bureau, an empty chair sits facing the bed. And on the wall directly above the chair, a familiar print. Blobby flowers in two white vases. I turn to look at Min to make sure she sees it, too. It's the same print as the ones in our room.

The other photo shows a white sink with bloodstains around the edges. Above it is a mirror. Written on it in thick white letters is *LET THIS BE A LESSON*.

I have to swallow hard to keep the junk food down. "Where did you get these photos?" I ask. "Did you take them?"

Instead of answering, Travis says, "There's an article toward the back that tells the whole story. Or at least what they know of it."

It's a newspaper article that's so long it takes up two facing pages of the album. People lean forward, but it's clear that only Knox and I are in a position to make out the words.

So I clear my throat and begin to read out loud.

14

HUMAN SACRIFICE

Friday, 11:48 PM

MYSTERY STILL SHROUDS DECADES-OLD UNSOLVED DOUBLE MURDER

An unsolved double murder still haunts a local motel. It's been over twenty years, and there are as yet no answers as to what happened at the Travel Inn & Out Motel on the night of September 13, 1996. The bodies of Gary Lockett and his mistress Jade Haney were found by a housekeeper in room 238. Blood was spattered across the wall, headboard, and carpet.

Both had their throats slashed, and Jade had also been stabbed in the heart. There was no sign of forced entry or a struggle, and it appeared that the two had been entertaining company beforehand. A chair sat next to the bed, indicating the killer had a conversation with them before the murder. The most unusual evidence was a message the killer wrote on the mirror with a carved piece of soap. Another twist? The motel had been hosting a morticians' convention that same weekend.

Thirty-six-year-old Lockett installed modems for the local cable company. Although he was married, he was rumored to date women he met through his work. That's how he met twenty-two-year-old Haney, who was a single mother of a two-year-old son. According to Haney's friends, they had been seeing each other for a few weeks when they planned a romantic weekend getaway a hundred miles away. But when the pair got to the motel, they learned it was hosting a morticians' conference, and there were no rooms available. Then the clerk double-checked and discovered a cancellation, which left room 238 available. Gary and Jade checked in at 7:40 PM.

According to some accounts, late that evening Jade argued with a bartender at the Tiger's Tail tiki bar, located inside the motel. Other than that, none of the staff or guests reported hearing or seeing anything strange that night.

At one PM the following day, a housekeeper tried to enter room 238 to clean, only to find it locked. She knocked several times but got no response. After obtaining the master key from the motel manager, she unlocked the door, took two steps inside, and began to scream.

Jade and Gary were lying faceup in bed, partially covered by blankets. Jade was fully dressed, but Gary was wearing only boxers. Blood was everywhere.

Authorities believe the crime scene indicated the killer knew his victims, as Gary seemed to have felt comfortable enough to have a conversation while lying in bed wearing only boxers.

Under the chair next to the bed, they found slivers of soap that had been whittled from one of the motel soaps. Whether the killer carved the soap before or after the murders, it's assumed he used the same knife to kill the victims. That knife has never been found.

After whittling the soap, he used it to write on the mirror. Authorities have never revealed what the message said. Then he washed his hands, wiped down anything he had touched, and left the room, with the TV still on and a DO NOT DISTURB sign dangling from the doorknob. It is believed he took with him a few small personal items that belonged to the victims.

No one has ever been charged with the killings, even though there were plenty of suspects.

Two months before the murders, Haney had kicked out her ex-boyfriend, citing his drug use. Afterward, he began to leave notes on her parked car when she worked as a waitress. She told friends that he often sat outside her house in his van. Haney filed a stalking complaint with the sheriff's department. At the time of her death, she was planning to move to escape his harassment. However, her ex-boyfriend had a solid alibi for the night of the murder and passed a polygraph.

As for the bartender Haney reportedly had a confrontation with that night, he left town the day after the killings. He abandoned his pickup in the motel parking lot and never collected his final paycheck. By the time authorities tracked him down, he had enlisted in the military and was in Germany. Later, investigators interviewed him and gave him a polygraph test. He said he was afraid that his lifestyle—he had been living in his truck—would make people think he was involved in the crime.

Lockett's wife had an alibi for the evening, but some theorized that a friend or family member might have taken it upon themselves to punish her husband for his cheating.

Others speculated about a local prison that has since closed, partly because of lax supervision that over the years allowed several inmates to escape. Could one of them have committed the murder on his way out of town?

And finally, there had been reports of cattle mutilations in the area attributed to cultist groups. At the time of the killing, authorities told the *Press Tribune* that the ultimate goal of these groups was human sacrifice.

After I finish reading and lift my head, there's a long moment of silence.

I think back to when we checked into our rooms. "Is anyone in our group in room two thirty-eight?" I'm relieved when everyone shakes their heads.

"They wouldn't be," Travis says. "When Stuart's folks were still alive, they never put anyone in that room. Now Stuart does sometimes, if people wanna pay extra."

Oscar raises an eyebrow. "Extra for what?"

His expression is curiously blank. "To sleep where two people died."

Raven's lip curls. "That's gross."

"I don't know." Knox shrugs. "I heard that Lizzie Borden's house is a bed-and-breakfast now. You can sleep where her dad and stepmom got whacked with an axe. People say they've seen their ghosts."

Min shakes her head. "I would not want to sleep where two people died. I wouldn't even be able to close my eyes."

"What about Gary and Jade, Travis?" Valeria asks. "Has anyone seen *their* ghosts?"

Travis treats the question seriously. "The day they died was a Friday. Friday the thirteenth. People say that's just superstition. But don't superstitions happen for a reason? Travis hasn't seen any ghosts, but sometimes things are in different places than he left them, or he hears a laugh, but when he turns around, no one's there. Stuart says that's just 'cuz this is an old place that's slowly falling apart. But when Travis walks past that room, he feels a cold breeze. Even though the windows inside are closed and locked."

We're all absolutely silent, caught up in Travis's spell. His weird way of speaking of himself in the third person just adds to the eeriness.

"And a few times guys in the Tiger's Tail have said they were talking to a beautiful blond woman all dressed in white, but when they turned away for just a second she'd disappear."

Maeve breaks the mood with a snort. "I think that's just called trying to lose a creep. They weren't talking to ghosts. They were talking to a girl who decided to get herself gone."

"Well, I don't want to talk about ghosts," Oscar says. "I want to talk more about the murders." His voice thrums with excitement. "Who do you think did it? The ex-boyfriend or the bartender?"

"That article was sexist." Valeria makes a face as she shakes back her hair. "It kept calling the killer *he*. Why couldn't the killer have been a woman?"

"Because that's not how women act," Min says, pulling a little apart from Valeria. "They don't stab people to death."

"Maybe not strangers," Valeria says. "I'll grant you that. Women aren't that kind of violent. But a woman who felt betrayed by one of them . . ." Her voice trails off.

"My money's on the ex-boyfriend," Raven says, "'cause it's always the current or ex-boyfriend. If a woman gets murdered, like fifty percent of the time the killer is someone she's been with."

"That makes sense, babe," Jermaine says, earning a squeeze of the shoulder from Raven. "That article says the ex was stalking her. He must have followed them to the motel. Seeing her with another man might have been the last straw."

Dev nods. "Especially if he was doing drugs."

As the conversation bounces back and forth, Travis turns his head like he's following a tennis match. But his eyes look dull, and he stifles a yawn.

"But what about the bartender?" I ask. That part of the article had caught my attention. "They must have had a pretty bad argument for people to remember it."

Adam leans forward. "How long have you worked here, Travis?"

"A long time. Couldn't find a job, but Stuart's folks were different. Let Travis do the things he likes, like cleaning."

"You've kept all those articles over the years, Travis," Adam says. "Who do you think did it?"

"Travis doesn't know. That why he keeps them. He looks at them sometimes when he can't go to"—he interrupts himself with a huge yawn—"to sleep."

And with that, the clock on the mantel strikes twelve.

He closes the scrapbook and stands. "Travis gotta get up in the morning. Already up way too late."

He doesn't say goodbye, but we all do.

Watching him go, Oscar says, "Maybe that's not a bad idea. Maybe we should all go to bed, too."

"I'd rather stay up all night than go to bed," Dev says.

"I'm not going to be able to sleep. Plus there's nothing to get up for tomorrow anyway."

"Except continental breakfast," Jermaine says.

Valeria has moved over to the bookcase. Now she grabs a box and holds it up. "Well, I'm not going to bed. Not when we can get all the answers we seek right here."

The box says OUIJA, MYSTIFYING ORACLE.

15

HUMANS ALWAYS SEE PATTERNS

Saturday, 12:08 AM

"A Ouija board?" Jermaine shakes his head. "Do you really want to open up that door?"

"Door to what?" Oscar asks.

"Evil spirits." He presses his lips together.

A few people start to smile until they see he's serious. It's just past midnight, and everyone's emotions are a little bigger than they would be during the day.

"Uh, it's just a game," Min says.

Jermaine leans forward, resting his elbows on his knees. "That's how they trick you. They say it's just a game. An innocent toy for kids. But it's not a toy. It's a fundamentally evil spiritual practice. It's basically just putting out a welcome mat for demons."

Adam makes a scoffing noise. "The whole thing is just a willing suspension of disbelief."

"Then how do you explain it giving answers?" Min asks.

"People want answers, so they see meaning where there isn't any. Or the two people with their hands on the pointer end up making tiny unconscious movements and working together without even meaning to."

"It's even more dangerous not to believe in it. Then you're just taunting it." Jermaine crosses his arms. "There are things you shouldn't mess with. And trying to communicate with the dead is one of them."

Valeria makes an impatient sound. "I'm not saying we mess with it. I'm saying we seriously and with respect consult the spirits."

Jermaine's broad face looks implacable. "Deuteronomy says you shouldn't practice divination, cast spells, or consult the dead. And here you all are thinking about doing exactly that."

He's revealed a side of himself I've never seen before. And judging by the way Raven is now frowning, it's new to her, too.

"Come on," Dev says. "Of course it's just a game. It's made by Parker Brothers. Does that mean you think if you play Monopoly, you can become a real millionaire?"

Jermaine doesn't answer, but his jaw works as he grits his teeth.

"Why do you have to take it so seriously?" Maeve says. It's more statement than question. She puts her hands on her hips. "We're just looking for something fun to do since we're all stuck here for who knows how long. You can go to bed if you think it's going to offend God or something."

"No, I'll stay." Jermaine lifts his chin. "If you're going to play with a spiritual loaded gun, you need someone present who understands the danger."

"Okay." Valeria claps her hands, undeterred. "First, we need one person to write down our questions as well as the answers the spirits give us. If it spells out a long word or a whole sentence, it's easy to lose track."

"I'll be the writer." Oscar raises his hand. "I can use that paper Stuart gave us."

"Okay," Valeria says. "Just be ready. Sometimes the letters spell out very quickly." As she speaks, she drags two dining room chairs to face each other in front of the couch. "Now we need two people to move the planchette on behalf of the spirits. It works better if it's a guy and a girl. Probably best if it's one from each team."

Knox sits down in one of the chairs. "I volunteer as tribute."

That means the other person needs to be a girl on my team. Min and Raven are all caught up with Valeria and Jermaine, respectively. So that leaves . . .

"Let Nell do it," Adam says. "She's the most level-headed. And if she runs into a bad spirit, she won't put up with any nonsense." Amusement edges his voice. It's clear that his skepticism is just as strong as Jermaine's belief.

"Way to represent, Mom," Raven says as I take the other chair.

"Don't we need a table?" I ask as Knox shoots me a grin and Maeve glowers.

"No," Valeria says. "You just rest the board on your knees. That way the spirit is working through your whole body, not just a flat artificial surface. And because it's working through both of you, your knees need to be touching."

Knox and I hitch our chairs forward at the same time. We bonk knees. He laughs and I apologize.

"Since you know all the rules, Valeria," Maeve says, "maybe you should be one of the people moving the planchette."

She shakes her head. "Actually, as the person with the most experience, I should be the medium. That's the person asking the questions."

"So only one person can ask questions?" Min says. "That doesn't seem fair."

"We'll take turns thinking up questions, but only one person should formally pose each question, so the spirits don't get confused."

No one else argues, since it's pretty clear she's the only person who knows the rules.

She continues. "Okay. To get the most effective results, everyone in this room needs to clear their minds and focus on the question at hand. We need to be serious and respectful. The spirits don't like ridiculous questions or people who laugh at them."

While she's speaking, Knox tips me a wink.

Almost reverently, Valeria opens the Ouija box. Inside there are just two pieces—the board and the pointer, or planchette. After unfolding the board, she balances it on our knees so it's facing her. On the top, it's printed with the word *Ouija*, as well as *Yes* on the left with a sun and *No* on the right with a moon. In the middle are the letters of the alphabet printed in two arcs, with *A–M* on the top, *N–Z* on the bottom. In a straight line under the alphabet are the numbers from one to nine ending with a zero. And underneath the numbers is the word *goodbye*. Only it's printed in all caps in two words. *GOOD BYE.*

The ivory-colored planchette is shaped like a teardrop, with a clear circle at the top. Valeria positions it so that the *G* shows through the circle.

"Okay, Knox and Nell, just rest the fingers of both hands very lightly on your side of the planchette." When we do, she says, "Now slowly move it around in a circle to get it warmed up."

It moves easily, feeling almost frictionless, as we move it clockwise in a circle slightly smaller than the board.

"Don't look at the board," Valeria says. "You don't

want to cheat without even meaning to. Look at each other instead."

Under my fingertips, the planchette starts to vibrate faintly, like the buzz of a single bee. I lift my hands. "Did you feel that?"

"What?" Knox looks impatient. "Put your hands back."

I reluctantly comply. I still feel it. "It's like it's buzzing or something." I think of the extra note about murder and death, how it felt like the piece of paper had hurt me.

His brows draw together. "I don't feel anything."

"We'll start with some warm-up questions," Valeria announces. "Questions that have short, simple answers. Like yes-or-no questions. So think of something you want to know, and when it's your turn, I'll ask on your behalf." When she speaks next, it's in a slightly louder and more formal tone. "First of all, thank you, spirits, for joining us here tonight. We are receptive to whatever words of wisdom you want to tell us."

Meanwhile, the planchette keeps circling. It feels like my fingers are following it rather than moving it. Does that mean Knox is directing where it should go?

"Nell, do you have a simple question for the board?" She is standing with her back to the fire, leaving her face in shadow.

"Spirits, will we get to our competitions?" The planchette doesn't change when I pose the question, but when

Valeria repeats it, it jerks toward one of Knox's corners. To the *No*.

"The planchette points to *No*," Valeria says to Oscar.

I examine Knox's face. Did he direct it? Or did we both just know the answer that has become increasingly clear as the night wears on and the storm shows no sign of ending?

"Start moving it again," Valeria instructs us. "Knox, do you have a question?"

Knox says, "Ask it if Elvis or Michael Jackson could speak to us."

She puts her fists on her hips. "I'm not going to ask that. It's disrespectful."

But the planchette had started moving before Valeria said anything. Again, the word *No*. Knox's eyes go wide.

We both must be moving it without meaning to, the way Adam said. We start the circle up again, but slower.

"Okay, Knox, ask a serious question."

He says, "How many spirits are in this room?"

After Valeria repeats it, the planchette slides to the number two. She calls it out, and Oscar writes it down.

"Maeve, your question?" Valeria asks.

"Are you good spirits?" Maeve lifts her chin as if to prove how brave she is.

After Valeria repeats the question, the pointer slides left, then right, then left again. I'm touching it so lightly that there's no way I can be moving it. It has to be Knox.

But when I look at him, his eyes are darting. He looks panicked. "No, yes, no, yes, no," Valeria reads out.

Oscar holds the pen poised over the pad of paper. "What does that even mean?"

Valeria tilts her head. "Spirits, are you saying one of you is good and one is bad?"

I've lifted my fingers to the point that just a few skin cells must be making contact as we circle the board. But still, I feel how the planchette strains to go. And then it does. Straight toward the word *Yes*.

The questions and answers come faster and faster.

"Are you the ghosts of the people who were murdered here?"

"Yes."

"Do we need to be worried?"

"Yes."

When it's Adam's turn, his tone is sardonic. It's clear he still believes this is just a game. "Spirits, is there something you want to tell us?"

"Yes." And then the pointer moves under our fingers faster and faster, darting from letter to letter, so fast that Valeria can barely keep up as she calls them out. "*H I C E T I A M S U M U S.*"

Finally it stops. My ragged exhalation is matched by Knox's.

"What did it say?" Min looks over Oscar's shoulder.

"Hi. Set I am sum us," Oscar reads out. "That doesn't make any sense."

"Spirits, could you please clarify?" Valeria asks. Then she whispers an aside to us. "Sometimes they don't like to be asked that."

Again the planchette speeds around the board so fast we can barely keep up. Valeria calls out, *"H I C E T I A M O C C I S O R E S T."*

And then the pointer goes still and slack again. Automatically, Knox and I take over, circling it around and around.

Oscar squints at what he's written. "Hi. Set I am oh scissor-ist?" His tone is questioning.

Thinking back to the newspaper article, I have an epiphany. "Maybe the spirits are trying to tell us that it wasn't a knife that killed Jade and Gary. Maybe it was a pair of scissors!"

Gasps. Nods. But then Adam rolls his eyes. "Oh, come on, Nell. Those letters are just random. They don't mean anything. Humans always see patterns, even when there aren't any."

"Why can't it be true?" Dev retorts. "Those were real people in that article. People who were brutally murdered maybe a couple hundred yards from here. If anyone has restless spirits, it's going to be them." And then he asks his question. "Is someone else going to die?"

I know I'm not moving it. I know I'm not. And I'm almost positive Knox isn't, either. All the playfulness is gone from his face as we both feel the planchette shoot to *Yes*.

"I don't want to do this anymore!" Min's voice trembles.

Raven snorts. "Adam's right. This is all fake; I need proo—" Before she finishes saying the word *proof*, there's a loud boom outside.

And then the lights go out.

16

DARK AS A GRAVE
Saturday, 12:47 AM

THE ROOM IS PLUNGED INTO DARKNESS.

I jump to my feet. The board goes sliding off my knees, taking the planchette with it. Good riddance. I want to get as far from that creepy thing as possible. I kick at the spot where I think the pointer landed but connect instead with someone's shin.

All around me, people call out. Some sound startled, others flat-out terrified. My heart is beating so hard it feels like it will burst out of my chest. The fire's flickering orange light turns people into black cutouts.

A flailing hand rakes down my cheek, scratching me. I don't know where I'm going, but I have to get out of here.

Blundering forward, arms outstretched, I almost immediately tangle with someone. She shrieks in terror, but I recognize her perfume.

"It's okay, Maeve," I shout. "It's just me. Nell." I don't know if she hears me over all the other noise, including the incoherent sounds she's making. We're just a mass of panicked people.

And then a cone of light cuts through the darkness. It's Adam's phone flashlight. A second later it's joined by a few others. The room begins to quiet.

"Do you think we blew a fuse?" Dev asks. He's standing next to the wall, batting the light switches up and down without results.

"I tried to tell you that the Ouija board wasn't just a game," Jermaine says.

"This is what happens when you demand proof." Valeria sweeps her light over the floor. "We made the spirts mad by doubting their very existence, so they knocked out the power. And to make it worse, we didn't even say goodbye to them. The doorway is still open. Who knows what will get through?" Her light picks out the board, which is under the couch. She grabs it, folds it in half, and tucks it under her arm.

"What did the spirits expect when they scared us like that?" Knox says. "So if we didn't say goodbye, it's not our fault."

Raven lets out a bark of laughter. "I hope you're not

suggesting we do it some more. It might only be a game, but it's one I'm definitely not playing in the dark."

Adam clucks his tongue. "Stuart told us when we checked in that the power was probably going to go out, and that's exactly what happened. A line got coated in ice and snapped, or the wind took down a tree or a pole. Losing power has nothing to do with that piece of cardboard and a plastic pointer. We're just lucky it didn't happen earlier."

I take a step closer to Knox, then stand on tiptoe to whisper in his ear. "Tell me the truth. Were you moving the planchette?"

"No!" he whispers back. His lips are so close his breath stirs my hair. "It was moving by itself. You felt it, same as me."

Oscar claps his hands. "Okay, team, whatever happened, I think it's a sign we should all just go to bed."

Dev laughs shakily. "Yeah, I think it's time to call it a night."

"Everything will look better in the morning," I say. It's what my moms always say, and so far, they've been right.

"I think we should just use one phone for light," Adam says. "We're not going to have any way to charge them until the power comes back on. Until then, they're basically plastic and metal bricks."

Oscar grunts. "Light and a clock are still pretty useful."

Before slipping my phone back in my pocket, I check the time. It's a little after one in the morning. I never stay up this late. No wonder I'm imagining things. This has been a long, crazy day.

With Adam in the lead, we all stumble down the hall, close enough that our shoulders, hips, and hands brush. We're like a weird beast with ten heads and twenty feet.

The corridor already seems colder. It's far from quiet. The wind howls, the floors creak, and occasionally a soft groan seems to come from everywhere and nowhere. It's definitely not human and must be a result of the motel resisting the gale-force winds, but it sounds like the moans of something alive.

We turn to the left, entering what memory tells me is the large carpeted area with the high ceiling, the concourse with conference rooms on either side that ends at the tiki bar and swimming pool. Not that we can see any of that. There's only Adam's cone of light slicing into the inky darkness. Without visible walls, I feel exposed. My shoulders are hunched around my ears. I keep one arm outstretched so I don't run into anything and hug myself with the other. I can't shake the feeling that something is moving in the dark corners, keeping pace with us.

Suddenly the Tiger's Tail looms up, looking even more fantastic and improbable than it did when the lights worked. We turn left and skirt the low white metal fence that surrounds the swimming pool. The windows of the rooms on our right distort our reflections.

Finally we turn right into the regular hall. I thought it

would be a relief to have walls and a ceiling close enough to touch, but instead it just feels claustrophobic. The ceiling seems lower, the corridor narrower. We reach the elevator, which of course we can't use, but next to it is a door that says STAIRS.

A hand touches the small of my back. I jerk away, stifling a scream.

"Sorry if I scared you," Knox says. "Isn't this where we have to split up? Our group is all on the first floor, and isn't yours on the second?"

"The second?" Dev echoes. "Does that mean you guys are by room two thirty-eight?"

"No," Adam says. "We're all in rooms that start with four. Which, this motel being what it is, are actually on the second floor." As he speaks, he opens the door to the stairwell. Inside, it's so dark it's like a black square.

"Well, good luck getting back," Oscar says.

Raven offers a little wave. "We'll see you guys at breakfast."

As Min and Valeria hug goodbye, Dev asks, "What time is breakfast again?"

"Seven to ten," I answer.

Maeve makes a scoffing noise. "See you at nine fifty-nine." While we've been talking, she's maneuvered herself closer to Knox. Now she offers me a smile while she slides her arm around his waist. In a little girl voice, she adds. "I'm getting all sleepy."

As the robotics team moves down the hall, Adam says, "Let's go up single file and keep one hand on the back of the person in front of us."

I end up with my hand on his back, and Min with her hand on mine. Behind her are Raven and Jermaine.

Once the door closes, it's as dark as a grave. Adam's light is trained ahead of him, meaning the rest of us are walking almost blind. The stairs are the metal kind with space between. A couple of times I catch a toe and head-butt his back.

I keep count in my head. On the thirteenth step, there's a landing. A turn, and thirteen more steps. When Adam pulls back the door, I hold my breath, as if there might be something on the other side. Between the story about the murder, the Ouija board, and my need for food and sleep, I feel like an exposed nerve.

Once we're out in the hall, Adam points his phone one way and then the other. "The problem is that I actually don't remember how we got to our room. Do you guys?"

The only other light comes from a couple of faint, glowing green exit signs that must run on batteries. It's impossible to tell how far away they are. They're so dim they seem to float in midair.

Raven shakes her head. "All I remember is that we were walking and walking and suddenly there it was."

This time we don't split up. I don't know about the others, but I feel like a zombie, just putting one foot in front of the other, stiff-legged, unthinking, dully watching Adam's light illuminate door after door, but never one that starts with a four.

And then we turn a corner, and his light finds a familiar number. But it's not one of ours.

It's room 238.

17

NEVER LOOK IN THE BATHROOM MIRROR

Saturday, 1:38 AM

STARING AT THE DOOR I LAST SAW IN TRAVIS'S SCRAPBOOK, I start to shiver. The hair lifts on my nape, and then a prickly sensation runs down my arms.

What lies on the other side of this plain, brown wooden door? It feels like at any moment it will swing wide and reveal...what? A bland empty room, the bed made up, just like our own? Or two lifeless bodies stretched out on the sheets, the killer sitting in a chair next to them while he leisurely carves a bar of soap with his red-streaked knife?

And suddenly it seems like I can smell blood, heavy and metallic, coating my tongue with salt and minerals. Trying not to throw up, I swallow hard.

"Can you feel it?" Raven raises her hands to trace the rectangle in the air. "It's like Travis said. Cold air is leaking from inside." When she stops talking, her teeth start to chatter.

She's right. It's like a chilly exhalation. It brushes my face and neck, stirs my hair the way Knox's whisper did earlier.

She raises her voice. "Spirits. We apologize for not treating you with respect earlier."

Jermaine says, "I rebuke you in the name of Jesus." He holds up his index fingers in the shape of a cross. His voice gathers power, until it's thunderous. "Get thee hence!"

"Stop it," Raven hisses. "They're not evil. They're victims!"

Min is looking even more shaken than she did downstairs, her hands jammed into her armpits as she hugs herself.

"You guys," Adam says, "it's from the storm outside. It's just the wind being pushed through cracks." He sounds like he's trying to convince himself.

"Come on." Min grabs my arm. "Let's get away from here!"

We hurry past. The hall seems alive with shapes and shadows. We turn and turn, and with each door we pass I brace myself for the sight of 238 again. But then Adam calls out, "Here's four fifty-four!" His and Jermaine's room is just two doors down.

Jermaine puts his arm around Raven's shoulders. "Hey, babe, me and Adam will stay with you girls until you find your rooms."

"We're fine." Raven's desire for Jermaine seems to have ebbed. "Now that we're in the fours, we'll be okay."

"But you're rooming by yourself," Jermaine says. "Is that safe?"

"You can bunk with us," I offer.

Raven raises her hands, finger spread wide, and shakes her head. "I actually think I'd do better by myself. Even for an extrovert, tonight's been a bit much."

Adam looks past at us. "Min? Nell? What do you want to do?"

I switch on my phone's light. It's 1:43 AM. "We'll be okay. And by morning, we'll be able to think about things more clearly."

"If you're sure," Adam says. "And now you know where to find us."

The corridor takes another jog and then we find 439, Raven's room. Before she goes inside, we insist on giving her a hug. I'd be scared, but she just enters without a backward glance. I hear her turn the dead bolt and then flip the metal swinging lock at the top of the door.

Now it's just me and Min. I play the light across door numbers, each one a single digit closer to our own. We take another turn, and suddenly we're back in the twos

114

again. After biting my lip so I don't start crying, I say, "Let's just retrace our steps and see if there's a different way."

And we do, and there is a branch we must have missed, and suddenly Min is sliding in the metal key.

As we enter, my hand automatically goes to the light switch. I've been longing to get here, but I realize all my half-formed thoughts involved light and heat, a sense of shelter from the storm. Instead it's pitch-black except for my phone flashlight.

The room smells of dust and the faint tang of mold. Outside, the wind howls. I realize I forgot to give Maeve back her sweatshirt. Earlier it had felt substantial, but now it's doing nothing to stop the cold from sucking at my bones.

Min's words underscore my thoughts. "I'm putting my coat on, taking my shoes off, and going to bed."

"You're not even going to brush your teeth?" That's not like Min.

"I've seen enough horror movies to know you should never look in the bathroom mirror if you're someplace that's haunted."

Setting my phone on the nightstand between our two beds so that it shines up, I manage a laugh. She's right. "Especially if the electricity is out." I hesitate. "When we were in front of that room, did you feel it?"

She toes her shoes off. "The air pushing out around the

frame? Yeah. I think Adam's probably right, that it's just the wind and an old falling-apart motel. But what about that Ouija board? Who was really controlling it?"

It's the question that's been rattling around in my head.

"I wasn't pushing it. I swear. I was barely touching it." I take my suitcase off the bed.

She puts hers on the floor at the foot of her bed. "Then Knox was."

"I don't think so. I was watching his face. He looked . . . scared." I sit down and untie my shoes.

"He likes drama, though. Pitting you against Maeve."

"Well, she's on his team, so she's got the advantage." I remember how I felt when I first saw him across the lobby, and I shiver again, but for different reasons.

Min grins. "Yeah, but you're the unknown quantity. Who isn't drawn to that?"

"So what about you and that Valeria?"

"She's cute, but I don't know. I think she really believed all that Ouija mumbo jumbo."

"I wish it hadn't said that someone else is going to die."

Min makes a scoffing sound. "It didn't say that. It didn't say anything. It was just a random string of letters, and then when Dev asked about someone else dying, you guys unconsciously pushed it toward *Yes*." She looks at me more closely. "You don't really believe that crap, do you?"

"I don't know what I believe." I put on my coat. "But those murders were real. And why wouldn't such a horrible event alter space or time, at least a little? Why shouldn't it linger?"

Min pulls on her own coat. "Maybe."

She and her shadow are making the same motions, but there's a second, fainter shadow, moving in completely different ways. It leans over the bed and raises its arm. And in the shadow hand there's a long narrow shape.

I gasp and put my hand over my mouth. As I do, the extra shadow disappears.

"What?"

"For a second, there were two shadows, not just one. And the second one looked like it was holding a knife."

Instead of looking frightened, she laughs. "You definitely need to go to bed."

"But I swear, I saw it." Stubbornness makes me clench my jaw.

Min sits on the edge of her bed. "Look. Everything always seems worse at night. And you've got a really good imagination. Plus you're exhausted. We had school today—I mean yesterday—and then you spent hours trying to keep us on the road through sheer force of will. You've had hardly anything to eat, and you're up way past normal." She grabs my hand. "It wasn't real. And this will all seem better in the morning. It's like those mass-hysteria events where a whole group of people becomes convinced there's a deadly chemical in the air, and they start passing out even though there isn't. That kind of thing is just as contagious as a real disease."

18

THIS IS THE FIRST

Saturday, 9:20 AM

MY EYES OPEN. OUR ROOM IS DIM, BUT IT'S CLEARLY MORNING. Light edges the curtains. In my dreams, I was... what? I remember running down a darkened hallway, but not what was chasing me. Just that it was awful.

Something's missing, though. And then I realize what it is. It's a sound, not a thing. The wind has finally stopped.

"Good morning, sleepyhead."

With a groan, I roll toward Min. She's sitting on the edge of her bed, dressed in the same clothes she slept in. She's put her shoes back on and pulled a beanie over her black hair.

"It feels like each of my teeth is wearing a little mitten."

My words create a fog that hangs in front of my face. Even under two blankets topped with the patterned brown polyester bedspread of dubious cleanness, the cold nibbles at me. And I can't believe I managed to sleep on the rock-hard pillow.

"That's what happens when you don't brush your teeth before bed." Min sounds annoyingly cheerful.

"What time is it, anyway?" I don't want to stick my arm out into the cold to grab my phone.

"About nine twenty."

"What does continental breakfast mean exactly?"

She shrugs. "Orange juice. And coffee, which I hope Stuart has figured out how to make without power. Sometimes it's just bagels and dry cereal. Sometimes they have stuff like yogurt or hard-boiled eggs."

Whatever it is, I can't wait to eat it. I swing my legs over the edge of the bed. While I'm fumbling on my shoes, Min opens the curtains. I stand up and join her in looking past the fringe of two-foot-long icicles hanging in front of the window.

It's stopped snowing, for now, but there are at least a couple of feet on the ground. Even though the sun is veiled by clouds, the light that leaks through is multiplied a thousandfold by the snow. We're on the back side of the motel, so instead of a view of the parking lot, it's just empty space blanketed with white. The wind has created drifts that look almost sculpted: mounds and hills, swells and slopes.

A few hundred yards away, bordered by a tangle of bushes and bracken, is a silvery line I think is a creek. On the other side, a dark forest begins. The snow-laden branches look like they belong in a fairy tale. But don't all fairy tales feature something evil? I shiver a little, but it's more of a fun shiver. There are much worse things than being cut off from the world when you have your friends, old and new, to play with.

In the bright light of day, everything that frightened me so much last night seems ridiculous. Overblown. The murders were years ago. The killer himself is probably long gone. As for thinking the planchette was moving itself, that had to have been Knox. Consciously or unconsciously.

A cold draft makes me hug myself. "Brr!" The window is the kind you can open. Even though it's closed, the gap where the pieces meet still lets in a lot of cold air. Which means Adam was right about the breeze we felt through the door to 238. I try to judge the weather. "What do you think? Is the storm over?"

Min, who understands the local weather, looks up at the sky. "I think it's just a break, not stopped for good. Besides, even if it doesn't snow any more, that kind of loose dry snow can still be dangerous. If the wind kicks it up, you can get all turned around and not have any idea where you are. Have you ever heard of the Children's Blizzard?"

I shake my head.

"It was in, like, 1888. They called it that because all

these kids tried to walk home from school but instead they just got lost and died. Some of the bodies were found only a few feet from their doors."

I make a raspberry noise as I comb my hair with my fingers. "Thanks! I was just starting to tell myself that my freak-out last night was irrational."

"It still was, because it was just your imagination. But the weather's real, and when you grow up here, you learn you'd better take it seriously."

When I open my phone, it's still a surprise to see *No Service*. It's 9:34.

"At least there's no point in trying to find the elevator," Min says. "Let's go down the nearest stairwell and hope we can figure out how to get to the common room from there."

Even though it's just as dark, the stairwell doesn't feel nearly as creepy as it did last night. And the first-floor corridor actually has some light, because opposite every stairwell there's an exit door with a window in the top half. I try to push open the nearest door. But it moves only a couple of inches before sticking on thigh-high snow.

"What are you doing?" Min says. "It's already cold enough in here without you making it colder." She grabs my wrist and pulls. "Come on. At least the common room has that fireplace." When we go around a corner, we spot Knox at the end of the hall, right before it opens up into a large carpeted space. He'd been looking out another exit door, but when he hears us, he waves and shouts, "Hello, strangers!"

My face breaks into a grin. I can't help it. In daylight and with bed head, he's still just as gorgeous. Good to know that at least one thing about last night was real.

"Look at that." He points outside.

I press my face against the window. He's not pointing at the snow, but what's on top of it. A dozen animal tracks. Each has four pointed toes above a bigger footpad.

"Are those from a dog?" I feel sick at the thought of it seeking shelter and finding none. "Poor thing! If it's out there, it has to be dead by now."

"No nails on the ends of the toes. Which means it's a cat, not a dog."

"A cat?" Min looks from her hand out to the tracks and back again. "Those tracks are as big as my palm."

"It's a mountain lion. Or a puma or a cougar or whatever word they use in California. They're all the same animal."

I take a step back. "In California, I think we usually call them cougars. But what was one doing so close to the motel?"

He raises an eyebrow. "Maybe it was hunting."

Living in LA, you'd hear about hikers seeing cougars, warnings to be careful with your dogs and toddlers.

Min's voice is small. "But mountain lions don't usually attack full-size humans, do they?"

I make a humming noise. Because I also remember reading about a cyclist killed in Washington and a hiker in Oregon. Both had tried to fight back—and lost. "Sometimes," I say. "But usually not."

"Well, it's out there and we're in here," Knox says, "so we're safe."

"That's all this place needs." I exhale sharply. "We get stranded by a terrible storm in a motel filled with creepy adults, unsolved murders, and even ghosts, and now there's a killer cougar outside. I cannot wait to leave."

Knox slips his arm around my waist. "Oh, really? And leave me behind?"

My stomach lurches, but this time with pleasure.

"All right, you two." Min's voice breaks the spell. "Let's go get some breakfast before they stop serving it."

Knox lets his hand drop as we walk out into the open space, where there's more light. I hadn't noticed them earlier, but large windows are set in the wall above the second floor.

We walk by the swimming pool and turn right at the Tiger's Tail. This part of the motel is starting to make sense to me. Next will be the conference rooms, then the lobby, and then we'll turn right toward the common room.

As I'm thinking this, Knox glances into one of the open rooms. A cry is torn from his throat. Suddenly he is running inside.

I'm still trying to make sense of what I'm seeing.

It's a conference room set up with tables and chairs, a white-tablecloth-covered table at the front for the speakers. To the left is an articulating wall that can be unfolded down the middle of the room to cut it into two. It's mostly folded up.

A rope hangs from the metal track that holds the top of the folding wall.

The rope ends in a noose.

And the noose is around a girl's neck. Her feet gently sway in the air. Her head is tipped down so that her bright red curls cover her face.

It's Maeve.

And pinned to her shirt is a note written in black Sharpie. In all capital letters it reads, *THIS IS THE FIRST*.

Someone won't stop screaming.

I realize it's me.

19

GUESS WHO THE KILLER IS?

Saturday, 9:29 AM

MAEVE SWAYS GENTLY. THE TOES OF HER RED CONVERSE ARE only about three feet above the floor, but it might as well be three miles. I press my icy hand against my mouth to stop the noise I'm making.

Dev shoulders his way between me and Min as he runs into the room. He wraps his arms around Maeve's thighs, hoisting her as high as he can, like a dancer lifting his partner. He's trying to take the weight off her slender white throat, but Maeve is unresponsive to his touch. She flops forward, head drooping and arms hanging loose. Maeve is literally dead weight.

Meanwhile, Knox has pulled over a nearby chair. In

one swift move, he steps up onto it while pulling a knife from his pocket. He sets it against the rope near her neck.

And suddenly she's loosed. The impact of her full weight sends Dev staggering and the two of them—the living boy and the dead girl—tumbling to the ground. After they land, Dev crabs backward, his face a mask of horror.

I finally find my voice. "I know CPR. Maybe I can"—I start forward, reviewing the steps. Look, listen, and feel. Thirty compressions. Two breaths. Repeat. I'm trying to reduce Maeve to a formula. To forget last night's laughing girl, the one who drew all eyes every time she opened her mouth.

Knox grabs my shoulder. "It's too late. I hate to say it, but she's . . . she's—" His voice breaks. "Her body's cold."

"And stiff," Dev says, his face still contorted. "Rigor mortis. She must have been hanging there for hours."

I realize that I'm unconsciously massaging my own throat. How long had it taken her to die, slowly strangling, her feet kicking desperately and finding no purchase, as her killer watched dispassionately? Or had she already been dead when the killer put a noose around her neck and hoisted her up?

A shriek at the doorway. Min is trying to hold Valeria back.

"No!" Valeria shouts. "This can't be happening! How can Maeve be dead?"

Knox yanks the white tablecloth off the speakers' table,

releasing a small cloud of dust. His eyes shining with tears, he drapes it over her body.

Someone is shouting for Stuart. The conference room, with its brown textured walls and lack of windows, is feeling smaller and smaller, almost claustrophobic. We could be underground. The way Maeve will be. I hug myself. Despite my coat, I can't stop shivering.

More and more people, adults and teens, are crowding into the room. But as if repelled by an invisible force field, they stay close to the door, well back from the body. Over and over, I hear Maeve's name and the words *hanged herself*.

They didn't see the note, so they don't know the truth, which is even worse. Maeve was murdered. And when I try to wrap my head around that fact and what it might mean for the rest of us, I can't. I can't think at all.

My group is mostly silent and stunned, while Maeve's teammates stumble, wail, sob. For once Oscar looks like an adult, his mouth a grim, thin line. Behind him, the other guests we met last night mostly just look confused, maybe even a little annoyed. I don't think they can even see Maeve's body from where they are standing in the hall. Only Travis appears frightened.

Wearing a dirty apron, Stuart pushes his way through the knot of people. When he sees the covered body, he freezes. Just his eyes move, going from the tablecloth to the swinging rope and back.

"That looks like a body. Who is it?"

"Maeve," Knox says, then elaborates. "The redheaded girl on our team."

"Did you check her pulse?" He takes a step toward her covered form.

"Yes. But she was already cold." Knox's throat moves as he swallows.

As a fresh wave of wailing breaks out, Mrs. McElroy shoulders her way in, carrying a half-eaten and fully forgotten bagel. When she sees the tablecloth-draped body, she turns pale. Her eyes dart around the room, checking to make sure that our team is all upright.

As Min grabs Mrs. McElroy's arm and explains what happened, Valeria says, "The Ouija board told us that someone else was going to die! But we didn't treat the spirits with respect, even though they tried to warn us. And now look what happened."

"Oh, give it a rest!" Adam says through gritted teeth.

Mrs. McElroy asks the same question we all have. "Are you sure she's dead?"

"She's cold." Dev still sounds shocked, like he can barely believe it himself.

"When was the last time anyone saw her?" Oscar says. "Valeria, you were rooming with her."

Her lips quiver. "She must have snuck out while I was sleeping." Her eyes are as flat and unfocused as a puppet's. "She's been so fragile lately. I should have reached out more."

"Maeve didn't kill herself," Knox says. "Someone did

it for her. They left a note pinned to her shirt. It said, 'This is the first.' "

Amid the cries of confusion and disbelief, Travis falls to his knees. "He's come back! The killer has come back!"

"Whatever happened," Min says, "we need to call the police."

"Remember?" Raven waves her dead phone, her voice cracking. "We can't call the police. We can't call anyone."

"What about that phone you had behind the counter?" I ask Stuart.

Stuart shakes his head. "It doesn't work without power. Even if we could get ahold of the police, they couldn't get here. The road's impassable. No one's getting in or out of here until this storm lets up. Before we lost power, they were forecasting more snow."

"And we just saw mountain lion tracks outside of the exit doors," Knox says. "Like it was looking in. So nobody should go outside."

Raven clutches her throat. "Because if we did, it could kill us."

Stuart waves her words away. "Don't worry about that. We've got enough real things to worry about without imagining trouble. Let's just stick to what happened here in this room."

"This isn't true!" Valeria's voice breaks. "It's just not."

Knox pulls her close. "I know that's how it feels, Val. How we all wish it wasn't true. But we have to accept it."

Valeria tries to squirm out of his grasp, but he won't let her go. Finally her shoulders slump, and she allows him to pull her close. He puts his lips against her ear and whispers.

Eventually she breaks free, her face set. "Okay. All right." She cuts her hand through the air. "I have to leave. I can't be here anymore."

Knox nods. "I think the rest of us should, too."

"What? We can't just leave Maeve alone," Jermaine protests. "It's disrespectful."

"What do you suggest we do?" Dev rolls his eyes. "Give her a good Christian burial?"

"Besides, we have to leave her here," Adam says. "The less we disturb the scene, the better. There could be DNA or fibers or other evidence. The more we touch her, the more we risk destroying it. In fact, we shouldn't even be in this room."

"I'm not going to touch her," I say. "But I do want to take a photo." As I start forward, Knox grabs my arm.

"Why in the world do you want to do that?" He sounds almost angry.

"I want to compare the writing on the note with the message written on the mirror twenty years ago—and from that one creepy slip from last night."

"I want to see it, too," Stuart says.

"Okay, but no one touch her," Knox says. "So we don't mess up the evidence."

After we edge forward, Knox slowly lifts the tablecloth.

My hands are shaking so much that I have trouble opening the camera app.

Maeve's face is partly covered by her hair, which is a blessing, as is the fact that her eyes are closed. She's wearing the same clothes she was last night—a tight black sweater and black knit pants—which doesn't mean anything about when she died, since I assume we all slept in our clothes. I realize I'm still wearing her sweatshirt. I guess I'll never give it back to her now.

The note safety-pinned to her sweater is in all caps. Just like the note in the mirror. Just like the slip of paper in our game. But I'll need to closely compare them to see if they're the same. I press the camera button. The flash in the dim room makes me jump, and some of the others cry out. Worried my shaking hand has made the picture blurry, I press the button again.

Something bothers me. It feels like there's a clue I'm missing, but I don't know what it is. A clue as to who killed her? Or why? Something feels so familiar.

Stuart stares down at her for a long moment. His jaw clenches, and his nostrils flare as he contemplates her corpse. "Okay. I've seen enough."

Knox gently drapes the tablecloth over her still form.

Stuart shoos us all out of the room, then closes the door behind himself and starts back toward the lobby.

As he does, everyone in the hall is looking at one another, as we realize that one of us must be the killer.

20

WE ARE STILL HERE
Saturday, 10:08 am

EVERYONE ENDS UP BACK IN THE COMMON ROOM. LAST NIGHT, IT was the place where we laughed and talked and clutched one another in fear or desire. The place we fled from when the lights went out. Now it's set up for breakfast.

Without any discussion, we kids take over the side of the room closest to the doors and fireplace, while the adult guests and Travis are closer to the windows. In between, Stuart, Mrs. McElroy, and Oscar stand deep in conversation. Oscar's not saying much. He rubs his temple as he stares down at the floor and listens to their low, urgent murmurs. Now he definitely doesn't look old enough to be a teacher.

Just as the adults are divided from us kids, we're divided from one another. My team is shocked, of course, but Maeve's friends are really hurting. Valeria wails Maeve's name, her face contorted. Min is trying to comfort her, but Valeria is having none of it.

Dev is just as quiet as Valeria is loud. He sits on one end of the couch, his face hidden against the upholstered arm, his back shaking. He's making a soft, rhythmic *heh-heh-heh* weeping sound that I can sense him willing to stop. Even though Knox is hurting, too, he is everywhere, shoring up his team. He goes from person to person, hugging them, squeezing their hands, whispering words of encouragement. He gets Valeria to quiet and Dev to straighten up. He confers quietly with Oscar. Seeing how they respond to Knox makes him attractive in a different way than he was last night.

Raven is once again in Jermaine's arms. The refuge she sometimes only pretended to need last night is clearly required now. She's hiding her face in his neck, her shoulders heaving. Looking helpless, he pats her back, murmuring, "Babe, babe."

Adam rakes his hands through his hair, so that it stands away from his face. His eyes are the color of gas flames, his cheekbones high and sharp. "I can't believe this is real," he says to me in a low voice.

Just standing feels like it's taking all my energy. My bones are like iron weights. I say, "I saw Maeve before they cut her down, and even I can't believe it's true. It feels like a horror movie. Or a nightmare."

"Or a character in a horror movie having a nightmare." One corner of Adam's mouth lifts in something that in other circumstances would be a smile.

"Too bad we can't just wake up or walk out of the theater," I say. "We're still stuck here."

The three other adult guests as well as Travis are on the other side of the room, looking about as lost as we are. Only Edgar seems unfazed, pushing a pink plastic tray down the stainless-steel counter. It now holds platters of bagels and muffins, a basket of Red Delicious apples so waxy they look fake, pitchers of milk and orange juice, and a cereal dispenser with Raisin Bran on one side and Froot Loops on the other.

Mrs. McElroy claps her hands. "Okay, people, quiet down." Everyone obeys her. She moves to stand in front of the fireplace. "Stuart tells me there is no way to alert the police as to what has happened here."

"I've been thinking about that," Jermaine says. "There has to be something we can do." He turns to Knox. "You guys know about circuits and computers and stuff. There must be some way to jury-rig an emergency radio or walkie-talkie or something. Some way to let people know we're in trouble."

A look passes between Knox and Dev. Knox says, "Sorry, man, for that you need electricity. Which we don't have."

Mrs. McElroy takes control again. "In light of that, we have to talk about safety. This room will become our base, and we need you to stick close to it."

"Aren't you ignoring reality?" Raven asks in a shaky voice. She points at the other half of the room, where the adults are gathered. "What about them? One of them must have done it. One of them has to be Maeve's killer."

We all look across the room. Travis, the handyman obsessed with murder. Brian, the trucker who likes sports and was looking for a cozy spot to read. Linus, the guy Knox's group picked up after his car slid off the road. And Edgar, the redheaded jerk who baited Dev.

All of them strong enough to strangle and string up a dead girl. And all of them looking back at us with varying degrees of dawning understanding.

Edgar says, "Don't look at us." He lifts his chin. "That girl was fully dressed. So if she wasn't raped, what reason would a stranger have to kill her? I'm thinking whoever did it has to be someone who knows her. Which means it has to be one of you guys, not us."

"That doesn't make any sense, either," Dev says. "Why would one of us do it?"

"Why does anyone kill anyone?" Edgar says. "Because they were mad or jealous or wanted to shut her up or something. And you kids seemed pretty loco last night. People tend to make bad choices when it's after midnight."

"But that note pinned to Maeve's chest looked like the

note left on the mirror after that couple was murdered," Min says. "Maybe the killer has come back."

Stuart clenches his jaw. "By the way, how do you guys even know about that?" But it's clear he's already guessed the answer, because he's glaring at Travis when he says it.

"Travis showed them his scrapbook," Travis says.

A thought, maybe a bit of memory, has been nagging at me. The words on Maeve's note remind me of something. But what? "What did that message written on the mirror say again?"

" 'Let this be a lesson,' " Travis repeats dully. "I guess we didn't learn it."

"He's come back," Valeria wails while Min tries to shush her. "He's come back to fulfill his promise."

"And it only took him over two decades." Adam's tone is skeptical.

Oscar puts his head in his hands. "This is all so wrong."

Mrs. McElroy pats his arm. "You can't monitor them twenty-four seven."

My thoughts flash through my brain like tiny iridescent fish. When I try to grab on to them, they slip away. The air beneath Maeve's feet. The pale column of her throat when she leaned into Knox. The sign on her chest. Her face only inches from mine when Knox held us. The noose around her neck. The way she held everyone's gaze last night. The red hair covering her eyes.

But then I finally catch a thought and manage to hold on to it. Right. I need to find the slips from our game. I can compare the writing on the note on Maeve's chest with the creepy slip about killing, the one that stung my fingers, the one no one claimed responsibility for. And after that, I can get Travis to bring out the scrapbook to see if any or all of the three things are written in the same handwriting.

I take the lid off the trash can. The smell—orange peels, old coffee grounds, and Doritos remnants—makes me gag, but I dive in anyway. I paw through the layers of empty Twizzler packages, crumpled chip bags, and candy wrappers, eventually hitting the coffee grounds that must be left over from yesterday's breakfast.

"What are you doing?" Min asks. "Are you okay?"

The slips are not there. Not just the bad one. All of them. The only piece of paper remaining is covered with capital letters written half in cursive that don't spell out anything but nonsense. The letters Valeria called out and Oscar wrote down. But there's nothing else.

"Earth to Nell," Dev says.

I straighten up. "The slips. The slips from Two Truths and a Lie are gone. I was going to compare the handwriting." I turn to Travis, even though I already know his answer. "Did you empty the garbage can?"

"No." He shakes his head. "That's where they went last night, though." He runs his hand down his little beard.

"What's missing?" Stuart asks.

"Those slips from our game. There was one extra with crazy stuff written on it, and no one would claim it. Now they're all gone."

"Tell him what it said," Raven says. "You're the one who drew the slip."

I turn to Stuart. "Okay, see, there are supposed to be two truths and one lie, right? The slip said that the person who wrote it had lost track of how many people they'd killed, that they didn't like mushrooms, and that they like to watch people die."

Brian sucks in his breath.

"Someone was just messing with you. That's all. Making kids jump at their own shadows," Edgar says.

Dev leans closer to the fire. "There's some burned bits of yellow paper in here. Someone must have burned the slips after we went to bed."

Linus points. "But then what's that piece of paper Nell's holding?"

"We were fooling around with this Ouija board we found. Valeria was trying to talk to the victims' spirits, but it just spelled out a bunch of letters that didn't make any sense."

Adam leans over me to look at the letters more closely. The color drains from his face.

"What? What's wrong?" I demand. Everyone is watching us.

He takes it from me. "It doesn't make sense in English. But it does in Latin. My dad insisted I take it, back when he thought he could turn me into a doctor." He clears his throat. " *'Hic etiam sumus. Hic etiam occisor est.'* " He sounds like a Harry Potter character casting spells.

"What does that mean?" Dev demands.

"Loosely translated it says, 'We are still here.' " He looks up with those incandescent blue eyes. " 'And so is the killer.' "

21

SUICIDE NEVER MAKES SENSE

Saturday, 10:20 AM

AMID GASPS AND SQUEALS, EDGAR MARCHES OVER TO ADAM. "Let me see that." He snatches the paper from his hand.

Adam doesn't resist. "Do you speak Latin?"

"No," he says, staring at the lines of scrawled letters. "I just know there's no way a bunch of kids playing around with a piece of plastic started getting messages from the dead. In Latin, no less." He barks a laugh. "I've heard stories about those two losers, the ones that were killed here. Both of them white trash. They certainly didn't speak Latin. They probably weren't that literate in English. It was always going to end badly for them. Car accident, drug overdose, shot by somebody who got jealous, beaten to death for telling the wrong person no. At least they got to die together."

"It doesn't matter what you believe," Valeria says. "All that matters is what happened. The spirits told us someone else was going to die, and now Maeve's dead. That's a fact you can't wish away."

"Look." Stuart raises his hands to get everyone's attention. His tone is edged with irritation. "Those murders were over two decades ago. Yes, someone killed two people here, and that ended up killing this motel. But whoever did it is long gone."

Mrs. McElroy sighs heavily. "Let's get back on track. The important thing is not what happened all those years ago. What's important is that right now there's a dead student in the conference room. It's not up to us to say who killed her. That's for the police."

"And how long is that going to take?" Edgar says. "Even in the best of times, when seconds count, the police are minutes away." Transferring the slip to his left hand, he reaches his other hand underneath the back of his loose sweater. "Right now, the only people we can count on are ourselves." As he says that, he pulls out a handgun and points it toward the ceiling.

At the sight of the gun, sleek and serious, there's a chorus of shrieks and exclamations. My heart is a trapped bird beating against the cage of my ribs.

"Put that damn thing away!" Linus raps out. He takes a

step toward Edgar, who is both taller and heavier. "You're scaring the kids!"

"*Scaring the kids.*" Edgar gives the words a sarcastic spin. "First of all, they're nearly adults. And second of all, I think real life is doing that all by itself."

"Everybody just needs to calm down," Brian says in a shaky voice.

"They're right, Edgar," Stuart says. "Put the gun away. You don't need to have it in your hand to be ready to use it."

There's a long moment where we all wait to see what Edgar will do. Linus is slightly crouched, his hands up, like he's ready to take matters, or at least the gun, into his own hands.

And just when it feels like the tension will snap, will end with another body lying dead on the floor, Edgar slides the gun into the back of his pants and pulls his sweater over it.

It feels like everyone in the room exhales at the same time. But anxiety is still electric in my veins.

Oscar scrubs his face with his hands. "This is all spinning out of control."

Knox puts his arm around his shoulder. "Remember, you have to be strong."

"No," Dev says. "We can't let this go on."

As he speaks, Valeria starts shaking her head. "We have to tell them."

"Dude, tell who what?" Jermaine asks.

Knox bites his lip. When he speaks, his words are halting, as if he has to search for each one. "Maeve had . . . issues. And she's been especially moody lately."

"Are you saying this might not actually be a murder?" Stuart raises an eyebrow.

"Maeve always liked to be the center of attention. And she's been pretty unhappy recently." Knox's voice gathers strength, as if he realizes there's no reason to keep her secrets anymore. "If she did kill herself, leaving that message might have been like her last middle finger gesture to the rest of us. She wanted us running around in circles and looking sideways at each other."

Dev sits down heavily and puts his hands over his face.

"That chair in the conference room wasn't that far away from her," I say, thinking out loud. "And she was suspended from the ceiling track that holds the folding door. What if she pinned the note on her chest and kicked herself away before she died? Tried to make it look like a murder?"

"I don't know," Min says. "That's pretty messed up."

Adam sucks in a breath. "Wait! I just remembered where I've heard that phrase before. 'This is the first' is from *The Mousetrap*."

The Mousetrap is probably Agatha Christie's most famous play. Even though I've never seen it, I know it's been running nonstop in London since the 1950s.

Mrs. McElroy's mouth falls open. "You're right. It's just

talked about, never shown." She knocks her forehead with her knuckles, as if jarring something loose. "The audience is told that a woman has been found with a note pinned to her chest that says, 'This is the first.'" She looks around at us and then at the snow pressing against the windows. "And in the play, a group of people are trapped at a hotel by a snowstorm. They're all suspected of being the killer."

There's a stunned silence as everyone tries to put the pieces together.

One thing still nags at me. "Where did Maeve get the rope to hang herself?"

"It might have come from the storage room," Travis offers. "Lots of odds and ends there. With an old place like this, you never know what you might need."

"But suicide doesn't make any sense," Raven protests. "Maeve seemed so happy last night. So alive."

Jermaine squeezes her shoulder. "Suicide never makes sense, but that doesn't mean it's not true."

Valeria marches over to Knox. "Last night, before we went to bed, Maeve couldn't stop talking about how you were flirting with Nell." Her eyes flash from his face to mine.

"What?" Knox puts his hand on his chest like he can't believe she's talking about him. "No, I wasn't."

"Come on," Dev says. "We all saw it."

Valeria wipes her tears with the heels of her hands, smearing her mascara. "Maeve was exhausted, she was sad, and she was probably imagining how great it would be to be the center of attention again. She's always been impulsive."

And then everyone's looking from me to Knox and back again. Like it's our fault Maeve is dead. I close my eyes rather than meet anyone's gaze. Even if I had nothing to do with it, it's being laid at my feet.

"It's up to the police to decide what really happened to Maeve," Mrs. McElroy says again. "Whatever the truth is, my top priority has to be your safety. I'm sure Oscar feels the same. Which means we stay together and we stay here."

He nods, looking miserable.

"You guys knock yourselves out," Edgar says as he finishes piling food on his tray. "I'm going back to my room."

"Don't let the door hit you on the way out," Brian says, his lip curling. He and Linus start talking in low voices while Stuart picks up an empty juice pitcher and disappears into the kitchen.

Mrs. McElroy returns to the rules she was making before. "If you want to go back to your rooms to retrieve your things, you need to take a buddy. In fact, I want everyone to pair up."

My eyes automatically find Knox, but he's already pulling Dev to his feet. "Come on, Dev," he says. "Let's go back to our room for a sec. I want to grab my suitcase, and you can get whatever you need."

Over Dev's head, he shoots me a look while mouthing, "Sorry."

I realize he's protecting me. If people think Maeve killed herself because Knox was flirting with me, then seeing us pair up will just make them more upset.

The only problem is that now everyone has a partner. There are the natural couples: Min and Valeria, and Raven and Jermaine. That leaves me, Adam, and Oscar.

"Uh-oh," Oscar says. "I guess I'm the odd one out." He hurries to catch up to Dev and Knox.

Adam leans in. " 'Mama always said life was like a box of chocolates. You never know what you're gonna get.' " He does a decent job of capturing Tom Hanks's accent as Forrest Gump.

I hope Adam doesn't think I'm disappointed. It's not like I *don't* like him. Without discussion, we move away from the group and to a corner next to a window.

When I start to say something, he holds up one finger. "Hold that thought." He goes over to the breakfast items and puts some baked goods on a plate, then pours a plastic cup of orange juice from the pitcher Stuart brought back out.

Min's plucking at Stuart's sleeve. "You don't even have a jar of instant tucked away someplace?"

"Sorry. And with no electricity, we're kind of stuck." He looks around the room. "If you guys need me, I'll be at the front desk."

"I'm going back to my room," Brian says. "But if you

want to get ahold of me, Stuart can tell you my room number."

I thought Adam was just making a plate for himself, but when he comes back he offers me a bear claw as well as the cup of juice. "You need to eat."

I wave it away. "I can't." Theoretically I should be ravenous, but instead I feel nauseated.

"Not eating can't bring Maeve back. Besides, we need to stay strong and alert. Something weird is happening in this place."

Giving up, I take the bear claw and nibble at a corner. It's so sweet and oily I gag. I force myself to swallow, and then say in a low voice, "What do you think really happened last night?"

"It's sad that Maeve killing herself seems like the best possible answer." Adam's mouth crimps.

"Did she seem down to you?"

He blows air through pursed lips. "Last night, she was the life of the party. But you and I are actors. We know that some people are good at putting on a different face when they have an audience."

"I want to ask Valeria more about what Maeve said. There's something about this whole thing that doesn't seem right to me." But when I turn to look for her, I see only Min.

Mrs. McElroy is deep in conversation with Linus. Taking my bear claw and juice, I walk over to Min, with Adam following. Keeping my voice low, I say, "Hey, where's Valeria?"

Min's reply is equally quiet. "She said she was going across the hall to the bathroom. I was going to go with her, but she got kind of annoyed." She glances in Mrs. McElroy's direction and lowers her voice. "She said she wasn't a little kid."

"But she's been gone for a while, right?" Dread weighs in my bones.

Min bites her lip.

"I think we should go look for her." I look at Adam. "Together."

22

WRITTEN IN BLOOD

Saturday, 10:48 AM

THANKFUL THAT MRS. MCELROY IS FACING THE OTHER WAY, I follow Min and Adam. We slip out of the common room before she notices that there is one fewer of us than there should be.

Adam waits in the shadowy hall as Min pushes open the door to the women's bathroom. I follow close on her heels. It's so dark inside that it seems to absorb the light of my phone flashlight.

Our footsteps echo as we creep forward. But all the stall doors stand open. Even though we walk down the line, it's pretty clear that wherever Valeria is, it's not here.

"Why would she want to take off without you?" Even though the two of us are alone, I'm whispering.

Min's mouth twists. "She said something about me not giving her enough space. Which is weird, because last night it felt like she was the one who was glued to my side."

I give her hand a quick squeeze.

"Sometimes things look different the next day," I offer. "But no matter how she's feeling, we still need to track her down. You don't want to risk making Mrs. McElroy mad for breaking the rule about staying with your partner."

We all shudder. Valeria can just waltz off without suffering much in the way of consequences, but Mrs. McElroy is our teacher. And you definitely don't want to get on her bad side. It's not that she yells or berates you. She doesn't need to. Just seeing her disappointed expression is punishment enough.

"Come on," I say. "Let's go ask Stuart for her room number and try to keep out of Mrs. McElroy's sight."

After we slip out the door, I put my finger to my lips and motion Adam to follow us down the hall. Once we reach the lobby, there's enough natural light that I can turn off my phone. Just as I had hoped, Stuart is at the front desk.

"Hey, Stuart, can you tell us Valeria's room number?" I ask. "She was supposed to stay with Min, but she took off on her own. We need to round her back up before Mrs. McElroy pitches a fit."

He gives us a conspiratorial look. "Yeah, we wouldn't want that." He pulls a big black ledger closer to him and leans over it. "You're lucky I still do things old-school. If it was all on the computer, I wouldn't have any idea." He turns back a page and then looks up at us. "Room three nineteen."

"Thank you." Min and Adam repeat my words.

"Remember that even though it starts with a three, it's on the first floor." He adds, "I hope she's feeling okay."

In unspoken agreement, we pick up our pace. We hurry past the closed doors to the conference room that holds Maeve's body, round the hulking Tiger's Tail, which looks even more surreal and dusty in daylight, and skirt the swimming pool.

The halls on the first floor are as much a maze as the ones on the second. I curse the lack of signage as we blunder up and down corridors that all look the same. Because of the occasional outside exit, there's some light, but not enough to easily read the room numbers.

I can smell the dust raised by our scuffing footsteps. I can even smell myself, the sharp tang of fresh sweat layered over old, despite the cool temperature in the hall. The mounting dread I felt earlier has returned, oozing through my body. The bear claw feels like it's alive and squirming in my gut.

"There!" Adam stops abruptly in front of the right number.

Min takes a steadying breath. "Valeria?" she calls, then raps lightly.

The door moves slightly under her knock. After shooting us a frightened look, Min puts her hand on the door and inches it open farther.

"Valeria?" Min's voice is softer now, as if she's afraid of waking her.

An open suitcase rests on the bureau. The door opens another inch, revealing the closed curtains. The ends of the beds come into view, both unmade.

And then the door swings wider still, and I see it. Blood. Blood all over. Smeared on the white sheets. Red spatters dotted on the wall, thick enough in places they have run. And most frightening of all, a single bloody handprint stamped just above one of the beds.

But no Valeria.

I want to be anyplace but here. At least back in the common room with everyone around us. Not here in the semi-darkness where clearly something awful has happened.

A moan makes me jump, fear zipping down my spine. When I turn, Min is starting to collapse, her knees buckling. Adam catches her just before she hits the floor.

"Check the bathroom," he says as he tries to haul her to her feet.

It takes all my courage to step into the room, to move through it, to turn the cold black metal doorknob. At first my sweaty palm can't get any purchase. I tighten my grip, grit my teeth, and push it open.

But there's no Valeria floating dead in a bloody tub or sprawled empty-eyed on the tile floor. Just a red-smeared sink that holds a pink-stained wet washcloth. In the mirror, my frightened eyes look back at me from someone else's head. The girl in the mirror is as pale as a ghost, with bed head and eyes that say she's about to lose it, big-time.

On the silvered glass, someone has written *THIS IS THE SECOND*.

A cold fist of terror squeezes my heart.

Because the words are written in blood.

23

A KILLER IN OUR MIDST

Saturday, 11:21 AM

I STARE AT THE WORDS IN THE MIRROR. *THIS IS THE SECOND!* My pulse thuds in my ears, and my vision goes blurry. Finally, I force myself to back away. One step, and then another. But even once I'm out of the bathroom, it's no better. Not with the dark rivulets that have run down the walls. Not with the bloody handprint that marks Valeria's last desperate attempts to survive.

"Is she in there?" Adam asks from the hall, his voice cracking. His arm is still around Min's shoulder, supporting her. But at least she's on her own two feet and her eyes are open. Open and watching me.

I shake my head. "But someone wrote 'This is the second' on the mirror."

Adam asks, "In soap?"

I really wish I didn't have to say the next part. "No. In blood."

Min makes a choking noise. Suddenly she leans over, braces her hands on her knees, and vomits. Adam's palm hovers over her shoulders, then he reaches down and gathers her dark hair back. I'm glad for the dim light, although it doesn't protect us from the sounds or smells. After a few seconds that seem endless, Min straightens up, wiping her mouth with the back of her hand.

"I wasn't sure that Maeve had killed herself. But this is definitely a murder."

"We don't know that Valeria's dead," I say without conviction.

Adam swallows hard before answering. "That's a lot of blood."

"Come on, Nell." Min's voice shakes. "Be realistic. Valeria's just as dead as Maeve. The killer murdered her and then, for whatever reason, hid her body." She blinks, and two tears roll down her cheeks.

That thought is even scarier than it would have been to see Valeria in the bathtub. Every time we open a door or go around a corner, we might find Valeria, staring back at us with dead eyes.

In our panic, it takes forever to figure out how to get back to the pool area. Every corridor and every turn seems to be the same, never getting us any closer. Outside, the wind is picking up, and the windows in the exit doors reveal only blurs of white. The windblown snow striking the glass sounds like the ghostly fingers of dead children tapping, tapping.

It feels like danger could come from any direction. We keep looking behind us. Keep flinching each time a corridor turns, forcing us to walk into the unknown. At one point, we end up again in front of the door to Valeria and Maeve's room, still ajar.

Adam starts to reach out to close it. Just before his fingers wrap around the handle, I grab his forearm. "Stop! There might be fingerprints!"

He nods, his face grim.

By the time we finally catch sight of the swimming pool at the end of a corridor, it feels like hours have passed.

Overcome with relief, we break into a half run as we go past the gently lapping water, the garishly painted tiki bar, and the closed-off conference rooms, including the one that hides a terrible secret. By the time we reach the lobby, the three of us are wheezing, sobbing, muttering.

Stuart's mouth drops open when he sees us stumbling toward him.

"Valeria's dead!" Min cries. "She's dead!"

His eyes go wide. "What? Oh my God! So you found her body in her room?"

"No," Adam says. "Just lots and lots of blood." He grimaces. "It was even on the walls."

I lean past him. "And written on the mirror was 'This is the second.'"

"So it's like the note that was on Maeve," Stuart says slowly, as the import of what we're describing dawns on him. "The same person must have killed both of them."

"Exactly," Min says.

Without saying anything else, Stuart disappears into his office. When he reappears a couple of minutes later, he's wearing a heavy red plaid coat. A black scarf is wrapped around his neck, and a backpack dangles from one shoulder. Tucked under his arms is a pair of snowshoes, the old wooden kind that look like oversize tennis rackets.

"I'm going to the police." As he speaks, Stuart jams a teal-blue wool hat down over his ears. It has a pom-pom on top, and tassels dangle from the earflaps.

"Didn't you say the roads are impassable?" I ask.

"For cars." He hefts the snowshoes. "I grew up here. I can cut through the woods behind the motel. There's a trail back to town. It doesn't parallel the road, but as the crow flies, it's much shorter. And right now, with all the roads turned to ice, it's probably the fastest way to get anyplace."

"Wait." Min's voice rises. "You're not going to leave us here all by ourselves, are you? With a killer on the loose?"

"I'm obviously not doing any good here." He yanks

on black leather gloves. "Me being here hasn't prevented someone from killing my guests. It has to be stopped."

"By the time you come back, we could all be dead," I protest, exchanging glances with Adam. He looks just as scared as I feel.

Our arguments aren't swaying Stuart. "You should be okay if you all stay together, like your teacher said. Tell Travis what happened and what I'm doing. He'll keep you safe."

And with that, Stuart walks toward the lobby doors. He stops in the space in between the two sets of doors and straps on his snowshoes. Then he turns, gives us a final wave, and marches out into the blowing snow.

Leaving us alone.

With a killer in our midst.

24

BAD TO WORSE

Saturday, 12:02 PM

"Oh God, oh God," I mutter as Stuart disappears. Even though he's going for help, it feels more like he's abandoning us.

Adam moves in front of me. His hands settle lightly on my shoulders.

I realize I'm hyperventilating, short, sharp breaths that barely reach past my throat.

"Look at me." His voice is urgent. "Nell. Look at me."

I do. His side-swept bangs reach past his eyebrows. In the cloudy light, the blue of his eyes seems more muted, the color of a still lake.

"Now breathe with me," Adam says.

Min moves closer. And then she and Adam start to take long, slow, nearly exaggerated breaths. I echo them. With each exhalation, my shoulders drop.

I'm starting to feel better, like a small creature that has found a hiding place. And then I remember. I'm not an animal. I'm human. Which means I can consider more than what is right in front of my face, even if what's there are my friends. I can remember the past. I can think about the future.

And all of it looks so dark. Maeve and Valeria dead. Stuart gone. The rest of us left to rattle around in the darkness in this creepy old motel, just waiting for the killer to strike again.

I step back, breaking contact. "We have to go tell the others what's happened."

When we walk into the common room, all eyes turn to us. Everyone but Brian and Edgar is there. And of course, Stuart.

"Wait—where's Valeria?" Knox leans forward to look past us. "Isn't she supposed to be with you guys, Min?"

"Valeria is dead!" Min's voice breaks. The faint calm we managed to find in the lobby is gone. "She told me she was going across the hall to use the bathroom, but instead she went to her room." Her voice rises with each word. "And somebody killed her!"

"What?" Mrs. McElroy gets to her feet. "That's why I told everyone to stay together."

"I'm sorry!" Min wails.

Jermaine looks stunned. "May God rest her soul."

"How do you know she's really dead?" Dev looks almost angry, like Min is lying. "Did you check her pulse?"

"The killer must have taken her body," I say. "But there's blood all over the room. So much blood." I can't help looking at Travis. "And someone wrote in blood on the mirror. It said, 'This is the second.'"

Travis starts to moan, rocking back and forth. He slaps the sides of his head with open hands, softly at first and then harder and harder. "It's happening again!"

Raven grabs one wrist, and then Jermaine grabs the other.

"Stop it, Travis," she says. "Hurting yourself is not going to help."

Oscar sounds stunned. "Just because there's blood and a note doesn't mean Valeria is dead."

Adam's voice is matter-of-fact, making his words even more awful. "There was so much blood it was running down the walls."

Raven claps a hand over her mouth.

Linus straightens up from where he's been leaning against the wall. "Blood can look like a lot more than it really is. I learned that in Iraq. Just a half cup of blood can cover a couple of square feet. It looks like gallons. But the Red Cross takes four times that amount just for a blood donation."

Dev crosses his arms. "Did you look under the bed to see if she was there? Did you check the closet?"

Min, Adam, and I exchange glances. We didn't do any of those things. Maybe Valeria's body is still in the room. And maybe—maybe she's not even dead. I remember that feeling I had in the lobby. Maybe she's found a place to hide from the killer.

"We were freaked out." A faint hope pulses in me. "We left in a hurry."

"Well, someone has to go back and check," Oscar says. "What if she's just injured and needs help?"

We all go together, including the remaining adults. Linus and Mrs. McElroy lead the way, while Travis and Oscar bring up the rear, with us students in the middle.

"When was the last time anyone saw Brian or Edgar?" Adam asks as we walk down the dim corridor.

There's a brief silence. Are they beginning to think what I am? That Brian or Edgar must have done it? And of the two, my money is on Edgar, the redheaded jerk, not Brian, the book-and-sports-loving trucker.

"They both left early on," Jermaine says. "Edgar first and then Brian."

Telling the group about Valeria pushed everything else out of our heads. "We forgot to tell you," I say. "When Stuart learned about what happened, he left. He's going to snowshoe into town and get the police."

Dev, who has been walking in front of me, halts so

abruptly that I bump into him. "Stuart left? Knox—we have to stop him!" Like me, he must see Stuart as the knowledgeable adult, the one who can best protect us. I remember Stuart slipping from shadow to shadow in the darkened hall, ready to attack my imaginary monster. If there's a murderer on the loose, Stuart's the one I want by my side.

Knox rubs his eyes, looking irritated. "You heard Nell. Stuart's already gone. And he's got snowshoes and we don't. But he's lived here most of his life. He knows what he's doing." The confidence that seemed so attractive last night is less enchanting today.

"This weekend keeps going from bad to worse," Oscar says. "This was supposed to be just a fun couple of days, with a little competition to keep things interesting." In the long run, he must think he will be held responsible for what happened to Maeve and Valeria.

"We're going to get in so much trouble," Dev says, then adds, "I mean we could. Without him."

Oscar mutters something under his breath that I can't catch. By now we're rounding the corner of the Tiger's Tail.

As we get closer, my footsteps start to drag. I don't want to go back. I don't want to see the blood-streaked room again. I don't want to find Valeria's broken body shoved under the bed or stuffed in the closet. Even if she's still alive, she must be really hurt. How will we be able to help her?

The sound of footsteps running behind us makes me turn. It's Travis, clutching his album to his chest. I hadn't even realized he was gone.

He falls into step behind me and pats it.

"To compare the notes."

It's a good idea. I just hope he doesn't have a complete breakdown when he sees the bloody writing on the mirror. Soap was bad enough.

Maybe it's because I don't really want to go back, or because it's marked by Min's vomit, but this time it seems like we find 319 easily.

The door is still ajar. I push to the front of the group, then wrap my hand in my sweater and nudge it open and walk a few steps inside. Most of the others hover in the doorway or stay in the hall.

"Oh my God," Knox cries as he follows me in. "The killer really has returned!"

There's something about the way he says it that catches my attention. Like he's trying to mask another emotion.

Like—like he's trying to suppress a laugh.

Which means—what? That Knox is really the killer?

No. That's not it.

I walk over to the window and pull back the curtains to let in more light. Then I reach out my index finger and run it down a rivulet. It's tacky to the touch.

"Ooh, that's blood!" Dev's upper lip pulls back. "Don't touch it."

"What are you doing?" Knox asks. "You're destroying evidence."

I bring my finger to my nose and sniff.

Blood smells like pennies. This smells like dessert.

And as everyone else shrieks or recoils in disgust, I stick out my tongue and lick my finger.

25

YOU SHOULD SEE YOUR FACE
Saturday, 12:21 PM

As I run my tongue over what seems to be blood, the color drains from everyone's faces—but for different reasons.

"What are you doing?" Adam yanks my hand away from my lips. "Nell, snap out of it!"

I thrust my fingers under his nose. "Smell it! It's stage blood! Homemade stage blood."

It was the faintly sweet smell that gave it away. Commercial stage blood is usually flavored with mint. This isn't. So it must be homemade. It's much cheaper, and it's also easy to make. All you need is Karo syrup, food coloring (not just red, but also a few drops of green and blue), and cocoa powder. Easy enough to whip up—at home.

Even though this motel has some sort of kitchen, it's the kind of place that just microwaves frozen food. Not the kind that would stock Karo syrup and food coloring.

Which means whoever put the blood on the walls must have brought the fake blood with them. My money's on Knox's group. But why would a robotics team pack stage blood? And then another piece falls into place.

Knox's showy laugh interrupts my thoughts. He points at me. "You should see your face!" He throws his head back in exaggerated amusement.

My own head feels like it might just explode. "You jerk! It's not funny!"

Anger fills me until my skin feels like it might pop. With a growl, I lower my head and run toward him. I put both hands on his broad chest and shove.

Knox's arms pinwheel. He loses his balance and lands with a splat on the bloody covers.

With the exception of Adam, everyone on my team is still looking lost. Travis and Linus look doubly confused.

But I'm focused on Dev and Oscar. I see the way they look at me and the way they look at Knox. When they meet my eyes, their faces are ashamed, embarrassed. When they glance at him, their expressions are filled with what I think is anxiety. Or fear.

So if this is stage blood, what else has been staged?

The answer is as obvious as the other death that supposedly happened today. Knox and Dev were the ones who cut Maeve down. The ones who declared her dead, who claimed that she was cold and stiff. And Knox was so quick to cover her up.

"What exactly is going on?" Min asks, her hands on her hips as she looks from me to Knox and back again.

"What's going on is that nobody's dead." I turn to Knox. "Right? Valeria's not dead, and neither is Maeve. You faked it all."

"Wait," Raven says. "They're not?"

"What?" Jermaine presses his fingertips against his temples.

I exhale as the full import of everything that has happened hits me. "These guys are drama geeks, just like us."

Knox tosses his head of thick dark hair, unrepentant. Last night, I wanted to run my fingers through it. Now I want to rip it out by the handful.

"Yeah," he says, "and we were robbed. We were supposed to be at the theater competition this weekend, same as you. Instead we're stranded at some rundown motel in the middle of nowhere. Other people are probably getting the applause and the awards and maybe even the scholarships we should have gotten. And we're stuck here."

"Why didn't you tell us the truth when we first met you?" Adam asks.

Knox shrugs. "It was a spur-of-the-moment thing. At first we were just having a little fun pretending, seeing if you would see through us when we said we were robotics nerds. But then, once you thought we didn't know any-thing, you guys were so full of it. Do you ever listen to yourselves? Boasting and bragging about how good you are. Just falling all over each other to explain the"—Knox puts on a hyperbolic upper-crust accent—"*th-ee-uh-ter* to us. So we decided that just because we couldn't make it to the competition, that didn't mean we couldn't compete. It started small. But after Travis told everyone about the old murders, late last night we decided to see if we could get you to believe people were again dropping like flies."

"You shouldn't joke about it," Travis says, his brow furrowing. "That's wrong."

No one pays him any attention, too caught up in other emotions.

"And guess what?" Knox says. "We won!" He and Dev exchange a high five. Knox starts humming "We Are the Champions."

"Wait? So there's no killer?" Linus's tone straddles incredulity and anger. When half a dozen people shake their heads, he throws his hands up in disgust. "I'm leav-ing. I'm sick of you kids. Talk about drama! There's too damn much of it. I can't wait until the weather clears up and I can get a tow for my car." With that, Linus storms out of the motel room.

Mrs. McElroy is staring at Oscar. I know that look. If you're the recipient, you can feel your soul shrivel. "So you knew about this?"

Not making eye contact, he hangs his head. "It was just a prank."

She shakes her head, disappointed. "An exceedingly cruel one. These are minors, Mr. Ewing. Children. And you have put their mental and even physical health at risk."

"It was a joke," Oscar says weakly.

"It was a joke, *and* it was a hyperlocal competition," Knox interjects. "But it had nearly everything that the real one did: technical challenges, improv, monologues, duet acting, group acting, even set design. We almost froze our butts off last night getting stuff out of our van. We had to work with what we had on hand, which was makeup, stage blood, a rope, and a jerk vest."

Jerk vests, similar to climbing harnesses, are worn under actors' clothes. They're called that because you can jerk actors in any direction you want, including making them look like they're flying. The rope that Maeve was suspended from must have had a cable threaded through it, clipped to a carabiner between her shoulder blades, the harness hidden by her clothes. In a stage hanging, the loop around the neck isn't actually part of the rope suspended from the ceiling. That way even if something goes wrong, there's no risk the actor will choke.

I'm the tech person for our crew, but even I have to admit that the illusion was complete. I had questioned only the provenance of the rope, not whether Maeve was really hanging from it. "But how did you hang the rope with no rigging?" I ask.

Dev proudly lifts his chin. "I got a spoon from the kitchen, used a door hinge to bend it, and hung the aircraft cable inside the rope from the point where the shaft met the bowl."

"Wait a minute," Min says. "Let me get this straight. You scared the daylights out of a bunch of people, and now you feel you've won some competition that is only in your little minds?"

Knox shrugs. "No blood, no foul."

"No blood, no foul?" Adam echoes. He makes a disgusted sound. "What about Stuart? He's out there right now risking his life to get the police."

"He'll be fine," Knox says, but with the least amount of conviction I've heard out of him today. "Besides, we would have stopped him from going if we knew it was happening."

Raven glowers at him. "What are you going to say when the police come? You'll get in trouble."

He waves his hand as if he can wave it away. "It was all a big misunderstanding."

"So where exactly is Valeria?" Min asks. I can tell by her face she is trying to decide just how angry to be with the girl who spent most of last evening in her arms—and to also decide how much of that was actually a lie.

"Dev, Oscar, and I helped her get the blood just right.

We flicked it off wet washcloths to make it look like blood spatter." Knox looks at the wall, admiring his work. "Then Valeria slipped into the conference room with Maeve while we went back to the common room." He takes out his phone and starts tapping on it.

"What are you doing?" I ask. "Wait—are you the ones who made it so we don't have cell service?"

He makes a scoffing noise. "No, the power's really out. But we all have a messaging app that doesn't need internet or cell service, just as long as you're close enough to someone who's running it. We use it at school, because once you're inside the building it's like a dead zone. If enough people have it on their phones, it works even better, because all those people together make a net that can relay the information."

He stares at his screen, waiting for a response.

And waiting.

There's no point in talking about what happened anymore. It was dumb, and it's done. We may be stuck at this motel with the biggest jerks on the planet, but at least we're safe.

It's a far different group that straggles down to the conference room to retrieve the two "dead" girls. We go in twos and threes. While we're no longer jumping at shadows, the mood's not much lighter.

"So you were pushing it, right?" I ask Knox. "The Ouija board?"

He shoots me an offended look. "Of course not. Whatever happened last night, I wasn't doing it."

When I roll my eyes, I don't bother to hide it.

I lengthen my strides to catch up with Dev. He doesn't look happy to see me fall into step with him.

"So you guys were just pretending to be our friends?" I ask.

"Look, I didn't want to, not at first. But Knox can be, um, very persuasive. When you're doing what he wants you to do, then he's the best. And if you don't want to do it? He has ways of still making it happen." His voice trails off. "Say you have a secret you don't want anyone to know about. Play along, and Knox will keep quiet."

Has he been manipulating his group the whole time? I run this morning through my head again. All those times I thought he was bucking up Oscar or comforting Valeria, was he really forcing them to play along?

When we round the corner, Knox is standing in the open door of the conference room, moving his phone flashlight from one corner of the room to the next. His mouth is open, but he's silent. For once, he is speechless. Adam and Oscar are standing right behind him. Oscar has his hand pressed tight to his mouth.

With my heart in my throat, I squeeze closer so I can see what's happening.

The room is empty. The tablecloth is again draped over

a table, not a still form. There's no Maeve. No Valeria. No one giggling and shushing each other.

No one at all.

Just a note written in thick red letters on the brown wall.

BETTER LEARN YOUR LESSON!

OUR ONLY SAFETY
Saturday, 12:42 PM

"WHERE ARE THEY?" MRS. MCELROY DEMANDS. "AND TELL THE truth, Knox, because I am fresh out of patience for this nonsense."

Instead of answering, Knox wheels on me. "Did you guys do something with the girls to get back at us?"

"What?" I welcome the red-hot anger boiling up in me, how it pushes aside the fear. I put my hands on my hips. "Unlike your group, we don't play those kind of sick games." Walking up to the writing, I sniff, relieved when I smell the same sweet scent I did in Valeria's room. "And this is more stage blood. They must be hiding someplace."

"But they're supposed to be here." Knox spins in a

circle. "And they definitely weren't supposed to write another note and then take off. Which means somebody took them."

"Oh my God," Min says. "The killer has come back. Just like the Ouija board said. And now he's killed Maeve and Valeria."

Adam makes a raspberry sound. "Didn't it say another person was going to die, not two? Besides, ghosts aren't capable of disappearing real, live people. Someone is just trying to make us afraid."

"If they're dead," Dev says, "where are their bodies?"

I feel whipsawed. The girls were dead, then alive, and now they're—what? Kidnapped? Hiding? Dead for real?

While we're arguing, Travis has opened up his album. He begins comparing the writing on the wall to the decades-old Polaroid of the bathroom mirror.

"There's no sign of a struggle." Adam waves his hand to encompass the room, which looks pretty much the way it did before, down to the rope still hanging from the ceiling. The only part missing is the loop that was around Maeve's neck. "I say you're still pranking us."

Oscar fists his hands in his hair. "We're not, I swear."

I would actually feel better if even just one chair was knocked over. If the tablecloth weren't again lined up perfectly with the table. Somehow the very neatness of the room feels ominous. Even a trail of real blood would give us a clue as to what happened here.

Jermaine stalks over to Knox. He's not any taller, but he must outweigh him by at least fifty pounds.

"Dude, give me your word that this isn't just another one of your so-called pranks that aren't funny. That you didn't tell the girls to write that on the wall and then go hide again."

"No." Knox puts his hand, fingers spread, on his chest, the picture of innocence, then raises it like he's being sworn in. "I swear to God I don't know where they are or what happened to them. I'm just as freaked out as you are."

Mrs. McElroy sniffs. "That and five dollars will get me a latte."

"Hey, Knox." Raven raises the back of her hand toward him, thumb and pinky tucked in, three fingers pointed to the side. "Read between the lines. If you hadn't come up with this dumb idea, Valeria and Maeve would still be here."

Knox takes a step back. "You can't blame this on me! It's the motel. It's haunted or there's a serial killer or both. But my team didn't do this."

"He's telling the truth," Oscar says. "We honestly don't know where they are." He glances at Min. "And I don't believe that a ghost or spirit is responsible."

A half hour ago, thinking about how Stuart setting out on snowshoes to find the police seemed at best a dangerous mistake. Now it's the one thing that might save us.

"We just have to stay safe and make sure nothing else bad happens until Stuart gets back with the police," I say.

Oscar shakes his head. "How do we know he'll make it? Even if he does, the cops might not be able to get back here."

"We need to find the girls now," Dev says. "They might still be alive, but for how long?"

"You guys keep acting like it's a stranger," Jermaine says. "But if this place is cut off, it has to be someone who's already here."

"Okay," I say, "if we take their team's word for it and they're not involved, then that leaves the other people who are staying here. That's Brian, Edgar, and I guess Linus. And Edgar and Brian left the common room this morning."

"Even Linus took off for a while," Travis volunteers. "And he's gone now."

Adam steps closer to Travis and lowers his voice, as if talking to a skittish animal. "It seems like both Edgar and Brian know their way around this place. How well do you know them, Travis?"

He shrugs. "Both of them stay here a lot. Edgar's a, what do you call it, a pharmaceutical rep. Brian's a trucker, same as Stuart used to be before his parents died."

"Do you think either of them could have done it?" Raven asks.

Travis shrugs and looks down at his boots.

I realize we might not be looking at the whole picture. "This motel is so huge. Travis, are there any other guests here?"

"Travis hasn't seen anyone else."

That isn't particularly reassuring. I remember Stuart checking the big black ledger. "There's a guest book at the front desk. We could see if there's more people than the ones we know about. And we can also get those guys' room numbers and make sure they're not holding Maeve and Valeria."

I think of Stuart's gun. But even if he left it behind, who among us could be trusted to use it?

"As I said before," Mrs. McElroy says, "our only safety is in staying together. So whatever we do, we'll do it as a group."

27

MUST NEEDS GO THAT THE DEVIL DRIVES

Saturday, 1:12 PM

BEFORE WE LEAVE THE CONFERENCE ROOM, I PULL A CHAIR UNDER the rope Maeve was "hanging" from. After a few vigorous shakes, the loop unhooks from the ceiling track.

Dev catches it as it falls. "What are you doing?"

"If we find whoever did it, we might need something to tie them up." He may be their tech guy, but I figure I have first dibs after the stunts they pulled. Stepping off the chair, I start pulling the aircraft cable—the thing that was really holding Maeve's weight—out of the top end of the rope. After coiling it around my fingers, I push it into my back pocket. To keep my hands free, I wrap the rope several times around my waist and tuck in the ends.

In a straggling line, we go back to the lobby. Travis walks behind the front desk. I follow more slowly, as do a few of the others. Raven brushes past me and goes straight into Stuart's living quarters.

"What are you guys doing?" I ask as Knox follows her.

She half turns and rolls her eyes. "Don't worry, Mom. We're not hurting anything. We're just looking."

"You guys." Travis looks anxious.

Unable to repress my own curiosity, I take a few steps inside. The main space is a living room/dining room/kitchen combo. In the center is a brown plaid couch and a TV. On one side is a range and refrigerator, and on the other a two-person dinette set. The bathroom is on the left. Through an open door on the right is a small bedroom, the bed made up with a brown striped spread. Everything is neat and impersonal. The only thing out of place is a bottle of Gorilla Glue on the dinette table.

Min pushes past the three of us and walks straight into the bedroom, where she opens the top drawer of the dresser. She stirs her hand through balled-up socks and folded underwear.

I move to the doorway. "What are you doing, Min?"

"Looking for his gun."

"Should you really be doing that? It feels like an invasion of Stuart's privacy. And besides, he probably took it with him."

She closes the drawer. My relief that she's stopping lasts only until she opens the drawer underneath.

"You guys!" Travis repeats from the doorway, wringing his hands.

I feel more and more anxious. "Think about it, Min. Do any of us besides Stuart and that creepy Edgar actually know how to fire a gun? We'd probably just end up killing someone on our side."

She doesn't pause. "Edgar having a gun is all the more reason we need one. He might be the person who took Maeve and Valeria. And what's that saying? 'Don't bring a knife to a gunfight'? We need to be able to fight fire with fire. Or at least look like we can."

Mrs. McElroy's voice from the bedroom doorway makes us both start. " 'Must needs go that the devil drives,' as the Bard says."

I'm not shocked that Mrs. McElroy is quoting from Shakespeare's *All's Well that Ends Well*. I *am* shocked that our teacher, of all people, is advocating for something that feels so wrong.

Five or six of us end up searching the rest of Stuart's living quarters. There aren't many places to look. I take the bathroom. In the medicine cabinet are mouthwash, rubbing alcohol, hair gel, and a couple of amber plastic prescription bottles. The only one I recognize is for Ambien, a sleeping pill. The wastebasket holds used floss, a toilet paper roll, and some curved scraps of red foam rubber. On top is a scrap that reminds me of a throwing star or maybe a drawing of a campfire with five tongues of flame. Something about it is familiar, but I don't have time to think about it.

In the drawers are the normal dental stuff, first aid items, toenail trimmers, and a half-used tube of Preparation H that both makes me wince and question again what we're doing. An old cigar box is tucked into the back of the bottom drawer. When I flip open the lid, there's a tangle of women's jewelry. Before I close the lid, I see a necklace with a Pisces sign, a drop earring with blue stones, and a man's plain wedding band.

"Was Stuart ever married?" I ask Travis after I come out. He's still standing in the doorway to the living quarters. Behind him, Raven and Jermaine are leafing through the black ledger.

He looks away, as if ashamed to be betraying a confidence. "He's always talking about the one who got away. About how she left him."

Everyone else ends up just as empty-handed as me. No gun under the mattress or the couch or on the kitchen shelves.

The only other place it could be is at the front desk. "Find any unknown names?" I ask Raven as I open the only drawer. But it just contains a jumble of pens and rubber bands and a single triple-A battery.

"No. Just the guys' room numbers." Raven finishes writing on the back of a *While You Were Out* slip. "Linus is

on the first floor, and Edgar and Brian are on the second."
She hands the paper to me.

Looking at the slip, I try to remember at what points during our game each of the three was in the common room. Could one of them have written the creepy note about killing? Or despite what he claims, could it be just another of Knox's sick jokes?

"Travis, where's the master key?" Mrs. McElroy asks.

For an answer, he pulls a ring of keys out of his pocket. "And Stuart keeps his in the desk drawer."

"Are you sure about that?" I ask. "I didn't see any keys."

"What are you talking about?" Travis opens the drawer I just searched. He stirs the contents, then looks up, alarmed. "It's gone."

I just hope that Stuart took it. Because the alternative makes me feel sick. A missing master key means the girls could be anywhere in this huge place.

The girls or their bodies.

And that no room is truly locked.

Mrs. McElroy has clearly come to the same conclusion. "While we're looking for the girls, we'll also get anything we might need out of our own rooms. Because once we get back in the common room, no one is going to leave it." Then she looks at Travis. "I'm afraid we should start with your room."

He starts back, his eyes wide. "Wait. What? Why?"

"Just to cover all our bases. You left the common room for a while this morning."

Instead of protesting, Travis turns and trudges toward the unmarked door he appeared from behind last night when we spilled into the lobby, laughing and relieved at having safely arrived. It's hard to believe that not even twenty-four hours have passed since then.

His space is so small that only Mrs. McElroy, Adam, Min, and I end up crowding in, while the others wait outside. The first part is a storage area filled with all his janitor stuff. Adam and Min use their phone flashlights since only a little light reaches from the windows into Travis's adjoining personal space. Their lights play over his yellow janitor cart, two rolling luggage trolleys, mops, vacuums, industrial brooms and dust mops, yellow plastic triangles that warn of wet floors, and stacks of new toilet paper as well as a basket filled with half-used rolls. Plastic shelving units are filled with rags, squeegees, tangles of extension cords, bottles of bleach and other cleaners, and boxes of paper towels and light bulbs. In the corner is a stack of paintings, exact replicas of the two in our room. It's decades of accumulated detritus, and there's hardly room to thread our way through to Travis's room.

His living area is only marginally less depressing. It's like the down-market version of Stuart's. A twin bed, neatly made up. The walls are bare except for some photos of colorful birds torn from magazines. Flamingos and parakeets and others so exotic that I don't know their names. His dining table and chairs are the same as the ones in the common room, only his are clearly the rejects, chipped, scratched, and dented. He's got a dorm-style fridge, a hot plate, and a microwave. Despite the window, it feels claustrophobic.

And even though Mrs. McElroy checks the closet and Min looks under the bed, there's no one in this room but us. Travis stands in the doorway between the storage space and his room, his head hanging low. He looks ashamed, and I feel embarrassed at even being here.

As we walk back out to join the others, Adam points at a door I hadn't noticed before. It's half-hidden by one of the luggage trolleys. "What's that?"

Travis says, "Stairs down to the mechanical room."

28

UNRECOGNIZABLE

Saturday, 2:03 PM

"I'M JUST GOING TO TAKE A QUICK LOOK," ADAM SAYS AS HE squeezes his way to the door.

He opens it, and I follow his bobbing cone of light down the stairs. At the bottom, he swings his phone's flashlight across a space filled with huge gray-metal electrical boxes and giant, round metal tanks that I think are boilers. Mysterious lengths of loose metal pipe rest on concrete blocks. More lean against the walls. Overhead, rotting insulation dangles from a tangle of pipes and duct. It smells of mold and decay. Somewhere ahead of us something is dripping.

"Maeve?" Adam calls out, and I join him, our voices strengthening as we repeat their names. "Maeve? Valeria?"

But there is no answer.

When we go back upstairs and out into the lobby, it's a relief to return to natural light and other people. Min gives me a wordless hug.

Next, we head to Linus's room, which is on the first floor. With Travis to guide us and the weak daylight that makes its way past the frosted windows of the exit doors, we don't get lost.

Mrs. McElroy calls Linus's name and knocks on his door, but no one answers. At a nod from her, Travis puts his master key in the door.

Watching him, I shiver. How harmless is Travis, anyway? Just as is true for whoever has Stuart's master key, he can get into any room at any time. Even if the girls weren't in his room, that doesn't mean he didn't put them someplace else.

Calling Linus's name one last time, Mrs. McElroy inches the door forward.

But the room is empty. No Linus, no Maeve, no Valeria.

"I wonder where he is," Dev says as he surveys the room. The bed is a mess of twisted sheets and blankets, but otherwise there's not much sign anyone has been here.

"This place is so big, he could easily have gone back to the common room without passing us," Adam says.

Jermaine opens the closet door wider. "No suitcase."

"He didn't have one when we picked him up," Knox says.

"Wait. What's this?" With both hands, Raven reaches past Jermaine toward the back of the single shelf. When she pulls them back, in her right hand is a red baseball cap. And in the left—

Min shrieks and scrambles backward. "What is that?"

It looks like a giant black spider the size of a dinner plate. Then I blink, and it resolves itself into a wig with two dozen shoulder-length dreads.

"It's a wig and a baseball cap." Raven reaches up again and retrieves a pair of sunglasses. Sunglasses. When it's been snowing.

I shoot Knox a confused look. "Was Linus wearing that when you picked him up?"

He shakes his head. "He wasn't wearing or carrying them. They must have been in his coat pockets."

I wonder if everyone is thinking what I am. That underneath the wig and hat and sunglasses, Linus would have been unrecognizable.

I can't come up with any explanation that is benign. Raven finally puts back what sure looks like a disguise.

I don't know if everyone is just as exhausted as I am, but we're mostly silent as we trudge from room to room, as Knox's team retrieves their things before we go to the second floor. They get their suitcases, as well as pillows and blankets. When we're done on the first floor, there's a mound of stuff sitting just outside the main hall, across from the pool.

Now for the second floor to check Edgar's and Brian's rooms. Once more, we go up the pitch-black stairway and into the equally dark hall. Only a couple of people use their phones, so we're mostly moving blind, taking short steps and bumping into one another.

It's the same confusing tangle of room numbers, which Travis cuts through unerringly. I keep an eye out for room 238, but we don't pass it.

When Mrs. McElroy knocks on Edgar's door, he answers right away. "What do you want?" He's standing in the doorframe, blocking the room behind him, so that we can't see inside.

"We just need to check your room," I say. "It's hard to explain, but it turns out that Maeve's not really dead, but she *is* missing. And so is another girl on Knox's team, Valeria. They faked their deaths, but then someone really took them."

"Spare me teenagers and their stupid games," Edgar says, rolling his eyes. "So now you think I might have done something? And you think Travis is on your side? That's rich." His words slur together, and his smile is bitter.

"What do you mean?" Oscar asks as Travis shrinks back, his shoulders curling over.

"Did he tell you the truth about himself? Did he tell you the real reason he keeps that stupid scrapbook?"

I lift my chin. "What *truth* is that?"

"There's a prison about five miles away. Back in the

day, Travis here was one of the prisoners. When he got out, he didn't have anyplace to go. Stuart's dad was too soft for his own good. He ended up taking him in to help out around the place." Edgar makes a sound like a laugh. "And that was only three weeks before those two were killed."

"T-T-Travis didn't do it," Travis stammers.

Edgar smirks. "And Edgar calls BS on that."

"What were you in prison for, Travis?" Mrs. McElroy cuts right to the chase.

"Fighting." His hand rises to the dent in his head. "The other guy hit his head and died."

"And you think I'm the bad guy and not him?" Edgar steps back. "You guys can go to town looking, but there's nobody but me here."

The curtains are open, revealing the room is a mess. It's strewn with clothes, food wrappers, an empty bottle of vodka, another one that's half-full, and a plate from the breakfast buffet. But there are clearly no girls stashed in the closet, the bathroom, or even (after Min lies down on the carpet to check) under the bed.

When we leave, none of us are in a better mood. Not Edgar and not us. And certainly not Travis. He's making a point of not meeting anyone's gaze.

After a few more twists and turns in the dark, we knock on Brian's door. He's been reading a book, sitting in the lone chair by the window, trying to catch the faint winter light. His room is neat. There's no one else here but him.

Brian left the book split open when he got up to answer the door, draped over the arm of the chair. Curious, I look closer. It's about four women spies during the Civil War.

As I straighten up, I glance outside. Only two pops of color break up the gray-and-white landscape. One is blue, the other red.

The first is a teal-blue winter hat tangled in the snow-covered canes of the blackberry bushes.

The last time I saw that hat, Stuart was pulling it on his head.

But the second splash of color is even worse. It's soaked into the snow, staining it scarlet.

Blood.

29

ALONE IN A UNIVERSE
Saturday, 3:13 PM

WHEN I GASP, MIN TURNS TO FOLLOW MY GAZE. "THAT'S BLOOD," she says. "And Stuart's hat."

"Oh my God, the killer must have gotten him." Raven puts her hand over her mouth.

"Maybe he's just hurt," Brian says hesitantly.

Knox cups his hands around his eyes as he presses his face against the window. "Or maybe that blood belongs to the bad guy."

Nobody says the obvious. That if Stuart hurt the bad guy and not the other way around, why hasn't he come back?

"Even if he's just hurt," Adam says, "he won't survive

long out there." He and I exchange a glance. I imagine we're thinking the same thing. If Stuart can still be helped, someone in this room needs to do it.

"Stuart had a gun," Oscar says. "And I'm pretty sure Edgar is not going to let us borrow his. That means we don't have any weapons."

Inspiration strikes me. "Maybe we do."

Abandoning the idea of retrieving everyone else's bags and blankets, we hurry down the stairs and back to the common room with the stuff that we've already collected.

The common room with its kitschy decor. Kitsch that can be repurposed.

Adam and Dev drag over chairs and start pulling things off the wall. They leave the paintings and photographs and signs. They even leave the rifle after Travis points out there are no shells for it. But the tennis racket, the cast-iron frying pan, the hoe, and even the rolling pin get handed down.

When Mrs. McElroy swings the tennis racket through the air, a piece of the wooden frame flies off.

Adam almost loses his balance on the chair as he wrestles down the old wooden sled with red runners. "If Stuart's hurt, we could put him on this and bring him back."

Dev hands down the ice skates, even though what we are facing is not ice, but mounds of snow. He shakes the oil lamp hopefully, then frowns. "It's empty."

"Too bad," Min says. "That would come in handy once it gets dark again."

Adam looks around. "Where's that weird thing that looks like a cast-iron pair of pliers made for a giant?"

"It's a pig puller," Raven answers definitively.

A few people snicker. Pull the pig is when you hook up with someone unattractive and make them fall for you.

She puts her hands on her hips. "For your information, it's for when a birth goes wrong and a piglet gets stuck. My uncle's a farmer."

"Well, whatever it is, it's not here anymore," Adam says.

What had been half-ridiculous becomes less so. The pig puller could definitely be used as a weapon. And why else would anyone want it?

We never vote on it or even nominate ourselves, but in the end, it's decided that Adam and I will be the ones to go out. At one point, Brian tries to say he should come with us, but we overrule him. It seems best for two people to go, and as nice as Brian seems, he's still a stranger.

When we walk back into the lobby, I'm wearing Raven's scarf, Min's gloves, Dev's hat, one of Knox's sweaters under Maeve's sweatshirt, Oscar's boots, and my own coat. I've left the rope behind. Adam is similarly attired in a hodgepodge of clothes. I've got the sled, and Adam the hoe, which he figures can double as weapon and staff.

Before we leave, I give Min a muffled hug through my layers of clothes. "Love you, girl," I whisper into her ear, feeling the weight and truth of the words. If we don't come back, I want her to know that. Her answer is a tighter squeeze.

Even in the vestibule it's freezing cold. Then I take a deep breath and push open the door to the outside.

The wind hits our faces like a slap, tearing away the white smoke of our breath. It's much stronger than it seemed when we looked out Brian's window. It pokes icy fingers into every gap, every buttonhole and cuff. It picks up grains of snow to sting our faces and patter against the glass of the doors behind us.

Leaning over me, Adam shouts in my ear. "We should do this fast, before the weather gets even worse."

Footsteps crunching, we climb the snowbank that slopes up from the lobby doors. But moving fast is out of the question. Stuart's snowshoes kept him from sinking, but our boots just punch through the snow. Clumsily, we follow the two furrows he left. The wind is starting to pick up the snow.

At first I try to step where Adam just did, nesting my smaller feet in his footprints, figuring he's already broken the ground for me. But it doesn't seem any easier than stepping onto unmarked snow.

When we round the corner of the motel, Adam points up at the roof. Icicles dangle from some sections. On others the snow has slid off the edge so that it hangs about a foot past it, suspended by nothing but air. It's beautiful and a little bit freaky and certainly nothing I ever saw in California.

We soldier on. The icy air burns my throat and lungs. It's so cold it feels like my chattering teeth might crack. The sizzle of driving snow hums in my ears as the frozen needles cut my face.

When we reach the back of the motel, Stuart's tracks turn away and strike through the field of white. They head toward the forested area, which is ringed by snow-covered blackberry bushes that look like lace. Stuart's hat is snagged on one of them. From here, we can't see the blood, or maybe it's been covered by the windblown snow.

After a few yards, I look back at the motel. It's hard to see, but I think I can make out figures behind one of the windows. I raise my hand in a wave. I can't tell if the motion is answered.

Step after faltering step, we slog forward. Sometimes the snow is up to our ankles, other times our hips. We keep on going toward the blue beacon of Stuart's hat, which the squall alternately reveals and hides.

The whole time, the sharp wind does its best to beat us back. The exposed skin of my neck and face feels seared, as if the air carries fire instead of ice.

The wind is also starting to smooth out Stuart's tracks. In fact, when I turn around, I find it's also erasing ours, filling up even the holes we sometimes leave behind when a drift is particularly deep. The motel is only a few hundred yards away, but it is barely visible as the gusts whip around it, lifting the snow into swirling funnels.

It feels like we are floating in a white silent world that is growing smaller by the moment. I brush the white pellets from my shoulders as others melt down my neck, making me shiver even harder when they trace my spine.

But is the wind just moving snow from place to place? Or is it starting to fall again? Panic flutters in my throat.

By now, though, we're only a few yards from Stuart's hat, caught on a waist-high tangle of blackberry canes. The new layer of snow does not completely hide splotches and splashes of red deep under the canes. I try to see the blood the way Linus might, as not that much. Just because it looks like a lot doesn't have to mean Stuart is dead.

At least I hope so.

Next to the blackberry bushes, the snow is all churned up from some kind of struggle. I imagine the killer following Stuart out here, trying to stop him from alerting the police. Stuart's hat coming off. A knife—the same knife that killed Jade and Gary?—slicing into him, spilling his blood. But where is Stuart?

Adam cups his hands around his mouth. "Stuart!" He's shouting, but the sound is nearly lost in the wind. Pinpricks of ice lance my clammy skin. Now that we're moving more slowly, the cold is sinking into my marrow.

Finally I'm near enough to pull the ice-rimed hat free. I cup one hand to block the wind and bend closer to the ground. There's a wide indentation where it looks like something has been dragged deeper into the bushes.

Or someone.

Then, under the shelter of the snow-covered bracken and brambles, I see them. A half-dozen tracks. Four toes above a center pad. The same ones we saw this morning. The tracks of a cougar.

And deep in the underbrush, there's one more clue. I stagger forward and tug it free. It's a scrap of thick fabric. Red plaid. I recognize the pattern. This piece of cloth is ragged, ripped from Stuart's coat.

And there's even more blood farther on, dark red against the snow.

It's only when Adam grabs my wrist that I realize he's trying to tell me something, the sound lost in the rush of the wind. I turn toward him. Ice feathers his eyebrows, webs his eyelashes, hangs in plugs from his nostrils. He points at the sky.

When I tilt my head back, fresh snow stings my face. It feels more like a sandstorm than a snowstorm. I hold up the ragged piece of cloth and point at the tracks.

He tugs my sleeve, his mouth moving. I can't hear all his words, but I know exactly what he's saying.

If we stay here, the mountain lion will get us, too. And the storm is getting worse. We have to leave.

We turn back, but it's like turning back into nothing. The air is filled with snow as fine as sifted flour. The sky is white, the air is white, the ground under our feet is white. Our tracks are truly gone now. Fear saps my strength. Are we even going in the right direction? After trudging for long minutes, I know we must be lost.

Lost. My mind tries to shove the word aside, but my body knows it's true. A cottony numbness is spreading through my limbs. Through my brain. We might be mere yards from the motel, but how will we ever know?

I remember reading about blizzards in the Little House series. Pa had strung a rope from the house to the barn, which didn't make sense to a kid in LA. How could you get lost in a dozen yards? Now, as we blunder forward, disoriented, blinded, I understand. I know how the kids trapped by the Children's Blizzard died mere feet from their doors.

Despite my borrowed gloves, with each passing minute my fingers lose more feeling. I have to look behind me to make sure I'm still dragging the sled. Adam is no longer using the hoe like a cane. Instead he just drags it through the snow.

My body is slick with sweat, but still the cold gnaws deep into my bones. If we make it out of here, I'm going to get the warmest clothes money can buy. The wind makes unworldly noises. It mutters and keens and sometimes sounds like distant shouts.

Or are those shouts real? Has someone ventured out to find us, the searchers becoming the lost? I imagine it happening over and over, would-be saviors turned victims, until finally the old motel stands empty.

Even though it's blowing straight into my mouth, the

wind is stealing my breath. Feeling suffocated, I stop, put my back to the wind, and round my shoulders, trying to suck in more air. When I turn back a minute later, Adam has disappeared. He's gone. I'm alone.

Cupping my hands around my eyes, I turn slowly to peer in every direction. The world is full of nothing. My chest goes hollow as the panic rises in me.

"Adam!" I shout. But I cannot hear my own voice over the roar of the wind. I am alone in a universe filled solid with small, stinging white streaks.

30

THE DEAD FOUND ANOTHER WAY
Saturday, 4:39 PM

I DON'T WANT TO DIE. AND I DON'T WANT ADAM TO DIE. BUT ARE those things really negotiable? I definitely don't want to die alone. I'm shaking from the cold, my teeth clacking together. As long as my flesh keeps jumping around my bones, my muscles will make enough heat to keep me warm. But the shivering is costing me, sapping my strength, my ability to care. The idea of lying down on the soft-looking snow, of surrendering, is so seductive.

My steps are getting shorter and slower, as it takes more and more effort just to raise my feet free of the snow.

A scratchy cry reaches me, and then another. A wordless protest.

A tiny burst of energy revives me. "Adam!" I shout. Has the killer found him?

Nothing but the wind answers me. Then finally there is another faint croaking call.

It's not Adam. I'm not even sure it's human. Still, I take one step and then another in the cry's direction.

When I was a kid and went hiking with my moms, they always impressed on me that if you get lost in the woods, you're supposed to stay put. But staying put in a blizzard means I could die. None of my choices are good.

I keep going, shuffling blindly, my hands in front of me. Every now and then, I hear another cry ahead of me. Around me, there is nothing but white. Except—has the quality of the white started to change?

The falling snow, I realize, is easing up.

And the sounds are getting louder. I swipe at my frozen lashes, trying to unglue them enough to see more clearly. An impossibly tall, slender shape looms in front of me, arms stretched overhead.

So many arms. It's a tree, limbs bare.

I tilt my head back. Four black ravens perch at the top, cawing roughly. Their agitation makes the branch bob up and down. Appearing in the middle of the storm, they don't even seem like birds, but more like powerful spirits come to warn me.

Four. Is the number really a coincidence? I think of Jude and Gary, of Maeve and Valeria. Have the dead found another way to come back and warn me?

A ghostly form takes shape on my left.

It's Adam. His face is dead white, except for two bright red spots on his cheekbones, the color brighter than anything I have in my makeup box. We embrace wordlessly, the ice on the fronts of our coats cracking. The wooden handle of the hoe thumps against my back, breaking off more bits of ice.

"Where are we?" he shouts over the wind. But I can make out his words, which means the gale is lessening.

"I don't know," I shout back. "We're just lucky we didn't wander into the creek."

Staying close enough to touch, we both turn in circles, hands cupped around our eyes, trying to locate any kind of landmark.

Past the tree with the four ravens, through the falling snow, I make out something. I squint. A long white box connected to a short dark box. A semi. I think it's the truck from our motel parking lot. Brian's truck. I nudge Adam, point, and then he sees it, too. It sits at about our two o'clock.

With renewed energy, we start toward it. Even though I still can't see the motel, I trust that it's there, somewhere past the truck.

Finally, we reach the back corner of the cargo box. In

unspoken agreement, we pause, savoring how it blocks the wind. The snow is not as deep on this side. Once we venture back out, it will be harder.

"Come on," I finally yell at Adam. "Just one more big push."

But before Adam can answer me, I hear a thump.

We both jump. Is it a branch breaking under the weight of the snow? I look around wildly. But there are no trees near us.

Another thump.

And now I pinpoint the sound.

It's coming from inside the truck.

31

BLOODY HANDPRINTS
Saturday, 5:16 PM

ANOTHER THUMP FROM INSIDE THE TRUCK, JUST ON THE OTHER side of the door. My heart leaps in my chest.

Adam and I look at each other, eyes wide. Someone is trapped inside.

"Stuart?" I yell. "Stuart!"

Two answering thumps.

No time to think about how he got in the truck or who locked him in there. We need to get him out of the freezing metal box and back in the motel. Get him warmed up and his wounds treated.

Each of the trailer doors opens with a metal lever that ends in a length of chain. The two chains are connected with a padlock. I cup the lock with my gloved hand, which is feeling more and more like a club, and look closer. It opens with a key, which of course we don't have.

Adam slides the handle of the hoe between the chain and the truck. He starts to twist it, putting torque on the metal links. Seeing what he is doing, I help him wind it until it's taken as many turns as it can. I can hear a few creaks and groans from the metal, but we need a way to torque it even farther.

"Archimedes!" Adam says. The wind has died down enough that he no longer needs to shout. " 'Give me a lever and a place to stand and I will move the world.' "

He turns the hoe and hooks the end under the bumper. It's supported by the chain. Then he puts all his weight on the end of the handle. I join him, pushing as hard as I can, my hands just below his. He starts to jump and I do, too, both of us jumping, pushing, and grunting. I just pray that the hoe handle doesn't break under our combined weight.

Finally, something gives way, but it's not the hoe, and it's not one of the chain links. It's the lock that snaps in the end, sending us tumbling back into the snow.

Adam scrambles up first. He reaches for the left-hand lever. He lifts it up and then pulls open the door. The frozen hinges protest with a groan.

But when it finally opens far enough for us to see who is inside, it's not Stuart.

It's a family. A mom, a dad, and what looks like maybe

an eight-year-old boy and a ten-year-old girl, all on their feet. They're wearing coats and hats and have gray quilted packing blankets draped over their shoulders.

The mom's hands are bare. Bare and bloodstained. And all along the inside of the truck door are red handprints marking where she must have been banging for help.

Worse yet, the boy isn't standing next to his parents. Instead, he's cradled in his dad's arms, limp against his broad chest. His head hangs back like a flower on a broken stem.

"*Por favor,*" the mother says. "*Por favor ayúdanos.*"

32

NO ONE IS COMING TO SAVE US
Saturday, 5:33 PM

I STARE AT THE FAMILY LIKE THEY ARE AN APPARITION. "DO YOU speak Spanish?" I ask Adam.

He shakes his head as he raises his arms to the dad, miming that he will take the boy.

I realize that of course you don't have to speak Spanish to know what they need.

Help. All kinds of help. Only some of which we can offer. But at least we can help them get inside the motel and get warm.

After the dad hands over the boy, he braces a hand on the truck's floor and hops to the ground. The mom helps the girl sit down on the end of the truck. The floor is even with my chest. I help the girl down, feeling how she shakes. Her black eyes are wide, her pupils dilated. When her cheek presses against mine it feels more like marble than skin.

"I think I might be able to put the mom and the girl on the sled," I say to Adam as the mom gets down. "Can you carry the boy?"

"I think so. But can you pull both of them?" He furrows his frosted eyebrows.

"I guess we're all just going to have to do what we have to do. The dad's going to have to walk, you're going to have to carry that kid, and I'm going to have to pull the mom and daughter. But it's our only choice."

I simultaneously explain and mime my plan to the family. At first the dad shakes his head. He even takes the boy from Adam, but after a few slow, struggling steps he turns around and hands him back. Adam gives him the hoe to use as a kind of cane.

Meanwhile, I help the girl sit on the sled, her body curled so that her knees are against her chest and her feet rest flat. Luckily, they're both petite, so the mom is able to sit behind her daughter, wrapping her arms around her and bracing her feet on the steering bar. After tucking one of the moving blankets around the mom's shoulders and under her butt, I grab the rope.

But when I pull, nothing happens. The weight from the two of them has sunk the runners into the snow. I grit my teeth and try again. Still no result. I'm pulling so hard the rope bites my skin through my gloves. Maybe I need to loosen the runners. I jerk the rope back and forth, then try again. I'm panting, but the sled is standing still.

I'm so tired. So tired and cold. If I were by myself, if other people weren't counting on me, I might just give up. Lie down in the snow and close my eyes.

Instead I lean back on my heels, so that I'm at a forty-five-degree angle to the ground, adding all my weight to the strength of my muscles. I grunt and strain, and finally the sled begins to move. But I can't keep walking backward. I manage to not lose momentum as I switch from leaning back to leaning forward. Adam is a few yards ahead of me. Behind him, the dad is relying more and more on the hoe with each step. We're a sad and sorry procession, shuffling slowly through the snow. When Adam stops to shift the boy, I keep moving, knowing I don't have enough strength to overcome inertia again.

It's probably only a couple hundred yards to the lobby, but it feels like miles. I plod forward. Under my gloves, my skin feels hot, like it's starting to blister.

A shout makes me raise my head.

"Nell!"

It's Min. She runs out and joins me in pulling the rope. And soon others are helping. Jermaine takes the boy from Adam. Knox slings the dad's arm around his shoulders.

Even though the heat's been off for nearly a day, once we get inside the lobby it feels as warm as an oven. Still carrying the boy, Jermaine runs ahead of us to the common room.

The other three can walk on their own, but they move slowly, their steps dragging. It's clear they've used up all their energy just keeping warm.

When we reach the common room, the kid is lying on the couch, still limp, his eyes closed. And Edgar, of all people, is leaning over him, taking his pulse. He starts barking orders.

"You two"—he points at Dev and Oscar—"lay out three blankets in front of the fire, one on top of another. We have to wrap this kid up, and also get extra clothes on the others. We need to get everyone warm inside and out. We need to have them drink warm sugar water and then give them something to eat. And most of all, we need hot-water bottles for this kid's armpits and groin."

Raven stares at him skeptically. "How do you know that's the right thing to do?"

"I hang out with a lot of doctors. And I snowmobile. You can get into trouble fast if your rig breaks down and no one can get to you for a while."

"How are we supposed to get hot water when there's no power?" Dev asks.

"Well, figure something out," Edgar snaps. "Maybe the kitchen has a pot or something you could put in the fireplace."

I head for the kitchen as Jermaine starts talking to the family. It sounds like he knows some Spanish.

Using my phone's flashlight to illuminate the gloom, Adam, Dev, and I start looking through the kitchen. You can barely call it that. It's clear not much cooking goes on here. There's a big freezer and a couple of microwaves to heat up items from the freezer. There's also a regular-sized fridge and oven. Adam does find a couple of large frying pans.

We fill them halfway with water. Dev's about to try to carry the first one out to the fireplace when my eye falls on the stove again.

"Hey, wait." Hope bubbles in me. "The stove is gas. Doesn't that mean it still works?"

But when I turn the handle, there's no clicking, no answering whoosh of flame. A few seconds later, there's just the rotting egg smell of gas. I turn it off. The last thing we need is to cause a fire or an explosion.

"It must have an electric ignition," Dev says. "If we had a flame, we could light it manually."

I go back into the common room, where people are going through their suitcases, giving the family new layers to bundle up in. Edgar has the boy wrapped up like a mummy next to the fire. "Does anyone have matches?" I ask. "I think we might be able to light the stove."

Knox digs a lighter out of his jeans' pocket and hands it to me. Oscar and Mrs. McElroy exchange a look. I'm sure that if today were yesterday, they would be lecturing him about smoking. But now no one says anything.

Back in the kitchen, the first burner I try lights. My

chest loosens. I light a second one and then put the frying pans on the stove. Not only can we heat water, but we'll be able to heat up food from the freezer. I turn to Adam. "Can you go see if you can find any water bottles or soda bottles with caps? We could turn them into hot-water bottles."

Five minutes later, I have filled two Coke bottles and a water bottle with hot water, while Adam has stirred more hot water into sugar in three cups. We bring them out to the common room. I only have eyes for the boy. His color looks better, and when Edgar loosens the covers to tuck in the water bottles, he begins to stir. Jermaine tells us the boy's name is Lorenzo. His parents are Reuben and Consuela, his sister Raquel. The family's last name is Salazar.

Consuela falls to her knees next to Lorenzo, tears rolling down her face.

Edgar gets to his feet. "A boy this age doesn't have a lot of body fat to keep him warm." He turns to Jermaine. "Tell the rest of them to drink up that sugar water."

Knox frowns. "Shouldn't someone strip down to their skivvies and get under the covers with the kid to help warm him up?"

Edgar shakes his head. "That's an old wives' tale. It's actually not that helpful for hypothermia. Those water bottles are going to help him better than anything."

Next, he turns his attention to Consuela, saying to Jermaine, "Tell her I need to look at their hands and feet."

Consuela sits on the end of the couch and hesitantly

holds out her hands. Edgar begins to examine them, turning on his phone flashlight. In the too-bright light, their color looks wrong. Too pale between the bloody bruises. And Consuela winces when he squeezes her fingers. Next, he has her sit down and take off her socks. He seems less worried by what he finds.

"Her fingers might be frostbitten." He shoots a glance at Knox. "Now, for that, skin-to-skin contact does help. Anyone care to volunteer their armpits?"

Jermaine translates for Consuela as Adam raises his hand. In an echo of Knox's lighthearted words last night, a time that now seems unbelievably far away, he says, "I volunteer as tribute."

Ducking her head and looking awkward, Consuela sits behind Adam on the couch. After he raises the hem of his shirt, she slowly snakes her hands under the cloth. When he yelps, she starts to pull them back, but then he clamps down his elbows, laughing and saying, *"Bueno, bueno."*

Edgar has been checking out the dad's hands and feet, but evidently they are okay. Jermaine is speaking softly with him.

"You've been a big help," Mrs. McElroy says to Edgar. He doesn't know it, but it's her highest compliment.

"Wait—I forgot to ask you guys," Min says. "What happened with Stuart?"

I've been so focused on the family that I had forgotten about the reason we originally went outside.

Adam and I exchange a look. I can feel the energy go out of the room as people guess that we only have more bad news. I wish I didn't have to say it, but finally I do.

"We found a lot of blood, a torn piece of his coat, and some cougar prints. To me it looked like the cougar dragged him into the underbrush."

Travis lets out a long, low moan. "You should have looked harder for him! What if he's just hurt?"

"Buddy, it started snowing so hard we barely made it back," Adam says gently. "And it's so cold out there. I don't see how he could survive without a hat."

Mrs. McElroy puts my thoughts into words. "So it's likely that no one is coming to save us."

Just then, Brian rounds the corner. "Hey, guys, what's—" He stops midsentence.

And Consuela pulls her hands out from Adam's shirt. She points at Brian as a torrent of angry words starts to pour out of her.

33

MURDER IS FAR-FETCHED
Saturday, 6:09 PM

AT THE SIGHT OF CONSUELA AND HER FAMILY, SOMETHING ABOUT Brian's face shifts. Or maybe it's that I can now see past his kindly, book-reading exterior to the darker interior. He swears softly, his jaw clenched.

Jermaine puts himself between Brian and Consuela. "They're saying you were supposed to be taking them to Chicago. But instead you left them in your truck during a blizzard."

Brian makes a scoffing noise. "It's not my fault that the weather turned and I had to make an unplanned stop. They had plenty of blankets back there, and they were out of the weather. I know from driving a big rig for years that the cargo never gets as cold as it is outside. Besides, they were pretty damned adamant that they didn't want to go back to where they come from. So what was I supposed to do with them?"

"You almost killed them!" I say. "Lorenzo could have died."

"They knew it was risky when they signed on. I can't guarantee the weather or that I'm not going to get pulled over by a cop or any one of a million other things that might go wrong. You can't blame the weather on me." He speaks through gritted teeth. "And they don't appreciate what a huge risk I'm taking for them. I could be thrown in jail just for helping them find a better life."

While he has been speaking, Jermaine has been translating, sotto voce, for the family. Now Consuela answers through him. " 'You're not doing it from your heart. You're doing it for money. Lots of money.' " Consuela rubs her thumb and fingers together as Jermaine speaks.

Edgar makes a noise halfway between a snort and a laugh. "So, Brian, you smuggle illegal aliens? And you're the one who's always giving me the side-eye."

"They're undocumented migrants. And you're one to talk. Half this state is addicted to opioids because of the drugs you told everybody were harmless."

Edgar suddenly deflates, his shoulders rounding. "That's what they said," he says weakly. "That's what we were told. That they were miracle drugs. They said they were nonaddictive."

"And yet you looked the other way when sketchy doctors started running pill mills open all hours of the night."

"Do we have to argue about everything?" Knox says. "Can't we focus on what's important?"

"And what's that?" Min asks in a weary voice.

"That Maeve and Valeria are still missing."

"Don't you care about what happened to Stuart?" Travis demands.

Oscar sighs. "We can't do anything about that."

"We can't do anything about anything," Adam says. "With Stuart missing, it's all up to us now. We just have to survive until the plows can get in and we can get out."

Mrs. McElroy addresses the other adults in the room. "The students as well as Oscar and I are going to spend the night here in this room."

Brian shakes his head. "Are you saying you're not letting anyone else in here? That you're the only ones who get access to the food and the fire? I don't think so."

She remains calm. "We're not stopping anyone from staying here. We're just saying that the only ones we trust are ourselves."

"So you think it's one of us?" Brian demands. "What— me, Edgar, Travis?" Travis starts at the sound of his name. "What about Linus?"

"He's gone and so is the pig puller," I say. "And we found a wig, sunglasses, and a baseball cap in his room. Like a disguise."

"What do we know about him anyway?" Dev presses his lips together. "Only what he told us. When we picked him up, he said he was on his way to visit his mother. But now I don't think that's true."

"What if some or all of them are working together?" Raven turns toward the three men. "It's clear you know each other."

Edgar exhales sharply. "That's pretty far-fetched."

"Yeah, well, murder is far-fetched," she answers. "And yet here we are."

I step forward. "I don't know if it's Linus or one of you," I say. "All I know is that I don't trust any adult except Mrs. McElroy right now." I look at Travis. "I'm sorry, Travis, but not even you."

He raises his chin. "Look, some people are just different. Not bad. Not evil. Travis was in a car accident; now he ain't the same." His Adam's apple moves up and down as he swallows. "Travis has his own room with its own lock. He can keep himself safe."

Watching him leave the common room, I think, *But can we?*

34

IMAGINE THE KILLER
Saturday, 6:40 PM

AFTER TRAVIS LEAVES, EDGAR AND BRIAN DECIDE TO GO BACK TO their own rooms as well. Before they do, they both rummage through the kitchen for food. No one says a word when they walk out with plastic trays heaped high. After they leave, we close the two sets of double doors. Dev helps me tie the handles together with the rope Maeve "hung" from. Now they won't be able to get back in if we don't want them to.

The sun is getting low, darkness starting to pool in the corners of the room. As the light dims, my mood does as well.

A gentle touch on my shoulder makes me jump. It's Adam.

"Want to help me see what we can make for dinner?"

I'm grateful for the interruption of my thoughts.

In the kitchen, Adam, Dev, Min, and I start rummaging through the cupboards, fridge, and freezer, checking out the contents with our phone flashlights. Adam and I try heating these microwavable "omelets" in the frying pans, but the pale flat triangles filled with neon orange American cheese stick and burn. The frozen hash browns fare a little better, as do the sausage patties. The meaty smell of them cooking makes my mouth water and brings more people—even some who I know for sure are vegetarians—crowding into the kitchen. It's cold enough that I can feel the warmth of their bodies, even the heat radiating from the blue gas flames.

We carry everything out on plastic trays, using them like serving platters. In the common room, the others have pushed all the tables together and circled them with the chairs. We set out the hash browns, sausages, the burned remnants of the eggs, and bagels with packets of cream cheese and jelly. There are pitchers of milk and juice as well as the industrial-sized boxes of cereal usually used to fill the dispensers.

As we pass the food around and load up our paper plates and bowls, Jermaine asks, "Do you guys mind if I say grace?"

People shake their heads or shrug, but most obediently

pause what they are doing, bow their heads, and close their eyes. I keep mine at half-mast.

"Lord, we thank You for this food. We also thank You for allowing us to find the Salazars."

At the sound of their last name, the family shifts in their seats. Jermaine quickly whispers a translation. Lorenzo still looks droopy, but he's sitting up without assistance.

Jermaine continues, "We ask that You continue to shield us from evil and bring us help as soon as possible. And most of all, we pray for Maeve, Valeria, and Stuart and that if it be Your will, You will keep them safe and sound. Amen."

His amen is echoed by the rest of us. When I glance over at Min, her eyes shine with unshed tears.

We eat in near darkness, the orange flicker of the firelight providing a faint illumination. Every now and then, a phone flares as its owner briefly checks something, while the rest of us wince, shielding our eyes like vampires confronted by daylight.

It's not much of a meal, but it's the best any of us have eaten in more than twenty-four hours. I feel my spirits rising with every bite.

When we're done, we clean up, nesting the disposable bowls, plates, and cups before throwing them away. We pile the pitchers and trays in the kitchen sink. Even though my phone shows it's just seven thirty, after all we've been through today, it feels like midnight.

"I think we should give the recliners to the family," I suggest as people start spreading blankets and bedspreads in front of the fire.

"I agree," Jermaine says in a voice that doesn't brook any argument. After Reuben and Lorenzo curl up in one recliner, and Consuela and Raquel in the other, we tuck blankets around them. Raquel's eyes shine in the firelight as she looks up at me.

Mrs. McElroy plops down on the couch. "I call dibs on the sofa."

"Wait. How come?" Knox says, or rather whines. I try to remember why I ever found him attractive. "Just 'cuz you're old?"

She gives him that stare we all know so well, the one that cuts to your core. "Yes, Knox. And I deserve something for being old. Goodness knows society doesn't give you much." She sighs as she stretches out. "And if old age has taught me anything, it's that when you deal with teenagers, often they will rise to the occasion. But sometimes they will disappoint you."

"Burn," Raven says smugly.

Mrs. McElroy's voice softens. "Look, I know we're all under a lot of stress. And underneath that, I'm sure you're disappointed that you didn't get to perform in front of your peers after you worked so hard."

Oscar chimes in. "The year our team went to state, I didn't win in any of my categories. Instead Jeremy Kohler walked away with damn near every prize. He did this scene from *The Laramie Project* that was so amazing that everyone started calling it *The Jeremy Project*. But I didn't mind," he continues, in a tone that clearly reveals how much he still resents Jeremy Kohler. "Theater has enriched my life and taught me so much. Besides, we all know that 'there are no small parts, only small actors.' "

The phrase is so familiar that people mutter the last few words along with Oscar. The darkness makes everything more intimate. Min, who is lying next to me, drapes her arm around my shoulders. Adam is on the other side of me, nearly as close even though he's on his own blanket. Adam, who almost died with me today. Who carried Lorenzo when even his father couldn't. Adam, who has always just been there, dependable and strong and practical, but who I never really saw before today.

"Do you guys ever have that nightmare?" Dev asks softly. "The one where you're onstage and it's opening night and everyone is watching and you have no idea what any of your lines are?"

"I have that dream all the time," Adam says. "Only I'm also naked."

After the knowing laughter dies down, Jermaine says, "Seriously, people, I don't think you appreciate how lucky you are to be part of this."

"So it's not the same with your sports posse or what-ever it's called?" Raven asks. She's sharing a blanket with him, so close that when I look over there's no space between them.

He laughs. "Babe, it's called a team."

"Right." Her tone makes it clear that the information is nothing she feels the need to retain.

"A football team is a family, like you guys are. But you all have accepted me in a way I didn't think you would. Plus in football, you practice every day so you can play thirty times. But you guys practice just as hard, and you only get to play—get it, *play!*—like, five times."

There are a few groans at Jermaine's bad pun, but not many. Someone who was once an outsider really gets us.

Dev's voice rises out of the darkness. "I actually played baseball as a little kid, if you can believe it. My parents made me do it. I was in the outfield picking dandelions and doing cartwheels. But then in fifth grade I got cast as an elf in our school play. That was all it took." There's a rustle as he gets to his feet. The fire lights up half his face.

He starts to sing, his voice soft but strong. It's "We're All in This Together" from *High School Musical*. After a few lines, Raven stands up and joins in. Normally hearing the cheesy lyrics would make me want to rip off my ears, but at this time and place, it somehow works.

When they finish, we clap by snapping our fingers, the way we would have at the competition. Now it serves the double purpose of not waking Mrs. McElroy. In response, Dev uses his fingers and thumbs to make the shape of a heart. Head tilted, he presses it against his own heart. Raven does the same.

Min makes a choking sound. At first I think she's crying, but then I hear what set it off and know it's really laughter.

Mrs. McElroy is snoring. Snores that are growing louder in volume.

"I wonder what's left in the little store," Min says in a stage whisper.

"I could go for something sweet." Knox rubs his belly.

"Or salty," Jermaine says.

I whisper-yell, "You guys! We promised that we wouldn't go anywhere except to the bathroom."

"Aren't there some more bathrooms down by the conference rooms?" Knox whispers, already getting to his feet. "We didn't promise which bathrooms."

Oscar says, "I'm going to stay here. And I think you should, too."

"If we go in a big group, we should be safe," Min says. "And it's only like a hundred yards away."

Jermaine starts to get up, but then Raven grabs him. "You have to stay here with me."

I'm not letting the rest go by themselves. So in the end, it's me, Adam, Dev, Knox, and Min. Moving as silently as possible, we gather up potential weapons—I take the rolling pin—undo the rope, and venture out.

It's not that far to the lobby, but my head is on a swivel, my eyes trying to pierce the darkness. My skin crawls as I imagine the killer watching us.

The adults must have thought of the little store earlier, because it is pretty picked over, especially now that the contents are basically free. The only stuff left are things that need to be microwaved, as well as Mike and Ikes, those chewy gummy things shaped like orange slices, Dots, and a single Hostess fruit pie, apple flavor. That doesn't stop us from gathering everything up.

Thinking of Stuart, I feel guilty. The only reason he had to charge five dollars for a small can of Pringles was because this motel is caught in a death spiral. And now he's probably suffered a terrible and senseless end trying to get us help.

"Hey, what's this?" Dev bends over and picks up something tucked next to the cooler. It's a bottle filled with garish pink liquid.

Adam leans closer. "Raspberry—oh, excuse me, *raspberri* with an *i*—flavored vodka."

Min says, "One of those men must have liberated it from the Tiger's Tail, then set it down when they came into the store and forgot to pick it back up."

"Or thought better of it." Adam makes a face.

Knox takes it from his hands. "Speak for yourself. I have a feeling this is the only thing that is going to allow me to sleep."

35

RESPONSIBLE FOR EVERYTHING
Saturday, 8:02 PM

BY THE TIME WE GET BACK TO THE COMMON ROOM WITH OUR bounty, we're weak with relief. As we tie up the doors again, most of the people who were sleeping start awake. When Mrs. McElroy realizes what we've done, she begins to lecture us, but then breaks it off in the middle.

"What's the point?" she says. "I'm just talking to myself. You kids always feel like you know better, at least until you learn it for yourself." To my surprise, she grabs the bottle of flavored vodka from Knox, twists off the top, and while I'm still trying to square her words and actions, tilts her head back and takes a long slug. Then she returns it to him, lies back down on the couch, and pulls a blanket over her head.

The bottle goes from hand to hand. Even Reuben takes a slug, despite Consuela shaking her head and muttering something in Spanish. True to the teachings of his church, Jermaine skips.

Next to me, Min takes the bottle that at least a half-dozen people have already drunk from. Watching her, I make a face. "What about germs?"

"What about them, Mom? This stuff is eighty proof. It will kill anything." She takes a big slug.

When she hands the bottle to me, I wipe the neck with the edge of my shirt. But when I raise it to my lips, it smells like chemicals, not berries. I lower the bottle and pass it to Adam.

His fingers touch mine when he takes it. "Reconsidering?"

"It smells gross. Plus it doesn't seem like such a good idea."

"I think you're right." Adam passes it on without raising it to his own lips. Pretty soon it's made its way full circle.

Coupled with everyone's exhaustion, the alcohol quickly makes people drop off. It's not long until the room is quiet except for the low crackle of the flames and a few snores.

Even though I'm so tired my eyes are burning, I can't follow the others into slumber. No matter what position I try, the floor, padded only by a bedspread, feels as hard as marble.

"Can't sleep?" Adam murmurs.

"No. I'm not sure it's even a good idea. Someone should keep watch."

He reaches out and takes my hand. He holds it loosely, but I'm aware of every centimeter of skin he's touching. We're both curled on our sides, facing each other, although I can't really see him in the dark. "You are not responsible for everything," he says softly. "Or everybody."

"If I don't worry about things, who will?" I'm one-quarter joking, three-quarters serious.

He's silent for a long moment. "You heard Mrs. McElroy. Even she's realized she can't control everything."

But letting go seems impossible. I still feel guilty that we allowed Stuart to leave, even though it was his idea and he's an adult.

Until now, I've thought that people calling me Mom was a term of endearment that recognized how I took care of them. But is it really a reference to all the negative views of moms? Of how moms worry, nag, and think they're the only ones with good ideas? Even my moms, who are great, at various times have done all of those things.

"What do you think happened to them?" I ask Adam. "The two girls." Min's sleep is restless, and I don't want to wake her up by using Valeria's name.

"Whoever took the master key could have stashed them in any room he wants."

"Who do you think did it?" I whisper.

"I would have said Edgar until we found the Salazars. Now we know Brian is capable of some pretty heinous stuff."

"What about Linus?" I ask. "We found that disguise, so we already know he was up to something bad. And now he's disappeared. Maybe he's holed up with the girls and the pig puller in another room."

Adam sighs. "I can't help feeling there's some kind of echo from what happened here all those years ago. Which maybe points the finger at Travis."

"He's certainly odd," I say, "but I have trouble picturing him as a killer."

"It's like there's a piece we're missing, but we don't know what it is."

I squeeze his hand but don't say anything. My brain is running on a hamster wheel of worries. Where is Linus? Could we have saved Stuart if we kept looking? What happened to Maeve and Valeria? What will happen to us?

When I wake up, it's still pitch-dark in the room. So it's not the light that wakes me. Nor is it a sound. Yes, a lot of people are snoring or at least breathing heavily, but it was like that when I finally drifted off. Min lies still on one side, and Adam on the other, so it wasn't a touch that roused me.

Instead, it's a smell. Or rather, two smells. The rotten egg smell added to natural gas. And layered over it is the smell of gasoline.

And a few feet from us is a fireplace full of flickering flames.

36

COLD AS KNIVES
Sunday, before dawn

I SNIFF AGAIN. I DEFINITELY SMELL BOTH KINDS OF GAS. THE PUNgent, almost sweet, chemical odor of gasoline layered on top of the rotting-egg smell the gas company adds to natural gas as a warning.

A warning, my brain repeats. I need to do something about it. About the smells and the fire in the fireplace. They're linked somehow, but it's hard to think. My head aches and I feel like I might throw up.

A phrase floats into my muddled thoughts. Carbon monoxide poisoning. Colorless, tasteless, invisible. It's why the gas company adds the sulfur smell. To serve as a warning. Because carbon monoxide can kill you.

Not only that, but gas fumes plus a source of ignition equals a bomb waiting to blow.

I push myself up on my elbows, ignoring the wave of dizziness that crests over me.

"You guys, wake up!" But the only answer is a groan from Adam.

When I shake Min's shoulder, she moves under my hand, loose and boneless. *Oh God, oh God.* Then I hear her take in a ragged, noisy breath. Almost like a snore.

"What's happening?" Adam mumbles.

"I don't know. All I know is that it smells like gas. Both kinds."

He swears. "The fireplace. What if it explodes? We have to put out the fire."

"And someone must have turned the stove on, so we've got to turn the burners off." What should we do after that? My thoughts slide away.

Once I'm on my feet, the sulfur smell is even worse. Tripping over bodies and sometimes stepping on them, Adam and I move toward the kitchen. Jermaine mutters a wordless protest, and I hear Consuela urgently whispering to Lorenzo and Raquel. I try not to think about how no one else says anything. No one else sits up.

As we reach the kitchen, the smell of natural gas is so strong it makes me gag. I'm careful not to even slide my feet. It feels like a single errant spark could send us up in a ball of fire.

All the burners are turned on full blast. We twist all of them off, but it doesn't make the air any fresher. Dizzy and nauseated, I try to breathe in the smallest sips.

"Only the people who drank that stupid raspberry vodka last night are having trouble. It must have been drugged," Adam says as he sets his phone on the counter, the flashlight shining at the ceiling. He grabs a frying pan and begins to fill it with water. "And now whoever drugged it is trying to kill us."

"But how did they get in here to turn on the gas?" I ask. "We tied the doors together."

In the back corner of the kitchen, between some wire shelves, I notice something I hadn't earlier. A door, set flush into the wall and painted the same color. It's ajar.

"Wait! What are you doing?" Adam says as I scramble over to it. I need to see what's on the other side, even if it's the person who tried to kill us. But when I pull open the door it just reveals an empty stairwell going down. I dart down a few steps and move the flashlight's beam over the space. It's a pantry, filled with bags of coffee and boxes of cereal, but empty of people.

Adam sighs in relief when I reappear. "Is there anyone down there?"

I shake my head. "It must connect to more of the basement." I think of the boiler room under Travis's space. Is there a whole network of rooms underneath our feet?

As Adam finishes filling a second frying pan, I drag a shelving unit in front of the door to block it.

It takes both hands to carry one of the frying pans filled with water, so I put my phone in my pocket. Back in the common room, I trip on someone and water slops over the edge. Adam's already started dousing the fire. I add the rest of my water. Now our last bit of light is gone, and we've added choking smoke on top of all the other toxic stuff in the air.

"Wha-what's happening?" Jermaine asks in a groggy voice.

"Someone is trying to kill us," I say as I make for the doors to the hall. I untie the rope holding them closed. But when I try to push one open, it sticks.

"Something's blocking the doors on the outside," I yell. I slam my shoulder against the door again and again, but it opens only an inch or two.

I hear Adam swing a chair against the window, but instead of the crash of breaking glass there's just a boinging sound. It must be shatterproof glass or even plastic. The sound is repeated two more times, but he's having no more luck with the windows than I am with the door. We're trapped in here with the toxic air.

I fall to my knees and snake my hand through the tiny vertical gap I created. Something has been wedged under the door. It feels like a wet towel. When I bring my fingers back toward my face, the gasoline smell gets stronger. The towel has been doused in it.

We have to get the door open. We have to get out of here before whoever it is—Brian? Edgar? Travis?—finishes us off the way they are clearly planning to.

I desperately pluck and wrench at the fabric, pulling a little bit more free each time, which allows the door to open a bit wider. Finally, there's enough space that when I get to my feet I can barely squeeze out, scraping my chest and hips between the door and the frame. Once I'm finally free, I pull my phone from my pocket and flick the flashlight on to make sure no one is lurking out in the hall, ready to kill me. Then I yank the towels loose—there's one shoved under each door—and pile them up.

I sniff again. It smells like more gas has been poured on the carpet. Even though I've opened all the doors, it is not really letting in fresher air.

The lobby seems impossibly far away. But at the other end of this short hall is a faint green light marking an emergency exit. I make for it. With no electricity, the alarm doesn't squawk when I push the door. It moves only a few inches before sticking on the snow. But the air that rushes in is fresh and clean, as well as so cold it feels like it's slicing into my lungs. Ignoring the pain, I take great gasping breaths. With no way to prop it open, I have to let the door close when I make my way back. I'm more aware than ever that the air smells like poison.

In the common room, Adam is already dragging Min out into the hall. Consuela is crying and tugging at an unconscious Reuben as her children do the same. Jermaine is trying to lift Raven, but he keeps tumbling down beside her and then struggling to his feet. Dev is sitting up and muttering, but he doesn't make any sense. Then he leans to one side and vomits.

Who should I grab first? There are too many people, too many people who are well on their way to being too many bodies.

And then I remember the luggage carts in Travis's space. With one, we could move two or three people at a time. That is, if Travis isn't the person who did this to us. If he's not waiting to kill off any stray survivors.

I grab Adam's sleeve. "I'm going to get the luggage trolley so we can move more people."

"I'll go with you."

"No. You're stronger. Keep getting people out of the room. I'll be right back."

His slow response tells me how much effort thinking costs him. "Then bring a weapon. In case they're waiting for you."

Reaching down into the fireplace, I grab handfuls of wet, greasy-feeling ash and quickly smear them on my face and hands. If our would-be killer is working in the dark, it will be harder for him to spot me. Then I shoulder the hoe and run out into the hall, dragging a chair behind me.

After wedging the emergency exit door open, I make for the lobby.

It's so dark that it wouldn't matter if I ran with my eyes closed. Moving on my tiptoes and trying to keep my breathing quiet, I find my way to Travis's space through muscle memory. When I open the first door, the smell of gasoline greets me. I risk turning on my phone. Under the door to his living quarters, the same rolled-up, saturated towel. So Travis can't be the killer. He's meant to be another victim, same as us. But I don't have time to spare to save him, too, not when so many of my friends need me.

Do I?

I compromise by yanking the towel free. I lean in his room and whisper-yell, "Travis—wake up! Someone's trying to set the motel on fire."

His answer is a groggy mumble. He sounds drugged, like the people back in the common room. But I can't spare the time to help him, not when every breath my friends take is filled with poison.

I find one of the trolleys and maneuver it toward the door to the lobby, turning off my phone flashlight before I open it. Holding the door open with my hip, I push the trolley out into the blackness of the foyer.

A flash of light behind me makes me wince. It's Travis. "Turn that off," I warn him as I let the door close again. "Someone out there is trying to kill us. They turned on the stove, blocked all the doors, and poured gasoline around.

My friends have all got carbon monoxide poisoning. I need the luggage trolley to carry them to fresh air."

He immediately douses his flashlight. "Okay. Travis will help you." There's a bang as he grabs the other trolley. We maneuver them out the door, and then we're both off, pushing the wheeled carts in a space darker than a child's nightmare.

I'm just getting up some speed when my trolley comes to an abrupt stop. It's run into something. But it's not a wall. It's not the front desk. When I walk around, I trip over the obstacle, barely managing to keep my balance.

What is it? I reach down and touch what feels like cloth with flesh underneath. A leg. Even when I squeeze it, it doesn't move or react.

I know it's not safe, but I have to know. Is it Maeve? Valeria? But when I cup my hand around the phone's light and turn it on, I'm staring at the back of someone who is not either of them. I grab the shoulder and half roll the body over.

It's Linus. There's blood all over his head, looking more black than red.

Travis has already disappeared around the corner, hurrying to the common room. I'm about ready to get up, about ready to push the trolley around Linus, when I spot something else.

A rectangular packet is hidden inside Linus's jacket. I look closer. It's a fat stack of fifty-dollar bills, banded like for a bank.

Not *like* for a bank. It must actually be from a bank. Now the hat, wig, and sunglasses all make sense. Linus must have worn the disguise into a bank when he was robbing it.

I remember what Knox said about Linus being desperate to get his car's trunk open. I know why he took the pig puller. He went back to get his loot.

And when he returned, someone killed him.

37

TOO LATE
Sunday, 6:08 AM

I STARE DOWN AT LINUS'S SLACK FEATURES. I CAN'T DO ANYTHING for him now. I have to remain focused on the living. Make sure they stay that way. After turning off my phone and tucking it in my pocket, I start to maneuver the trolley around his body.

In the darkness ahead of me, a soft sound makes my heart stutter. I freeze. It's a man breathing, the sound low and rough.

"Travis?" I say softly.

The only answer is footsteps. Sprinting straight toward me. Abandoning the luggage trolley, I turn and run. Away from the man. And, I realize too late, away from anyone who could help me.

A grunt. It sounds like he ran into something. The trolley or Linus's body or both. Is it Edgar? Brian? The sound was so short I can't identify who made it. It doesn't seem like it slowed him down.

I run with my hands outstretched, hoping that I'm hurtling straight through the wide concourse rather than at an angle that will send me into a wall. I picture it in my head, how it goes past the conference rooms and then narrows and turns at the Tiger's Tail, skirting the pool. Running on tiptoe, I try to keep my breath soundless, or at least as soundless as is possible when you're fleeing for your life.

I'm running away from danger. But I'm also running toward it. The air is starting to fill with choking smoke. It's coming from ahead of me, not behind. The guest rooms must be burning. My eyes sting, and I fight the urge to cough.

But I've got more immediate worries. Because the man's footsteps are still behind me. How can I fight back if—or when—he catches me? I left the hoe in Travis's workspace. I've got nothing.

Or do I? I remember the coil of wire in my pocket. If I wrap it around my fists, I could use it like a garrote. But doing that will require being up close and personal. Whoever it is, he is probably bigger and stronger, and he definitely won't have any qualms about hitting me or strangling me with his bare hands. And what if he has a weapon? Edgar has a gun, and Brian might.

Thump. My hip painfully grazes something big. Biting my lip to keep from grunting, I reach out to steady it, but it's so heavy that it's not wobbling at all. My fingers identify the carved surface. It's one of the big tiki heads. I start running again.

I sense more than see the looming presence of the Tiger's Tail on my left. I manage to avoid a second tiki head. In a few more yards, I'll have to turn left, past the pool, and then the only place to go is into the maze of rooms. And with every step, I'll be closer to the fire and farther away from anyone who can help me.

But what if I can make the killer think I'm someplace I'm not? I stutter to a stop, yank off one shoe, and toss it as far as I can. It lands with a muffled thump somewhere between the pool and the Tiger's Tail. As I had hoped, the footsteps run past me, toward my shoe. Still, I need to buy more time.

Dropping to my knees, I pull the cable around the tiki head, about a foot off the ground, thread the free end through the loop, and choke it tight. Then I scuttle forward looking for another tiki head. What I find first is a square metal support pillar. Working only by feel, I quickly tie a clove hitch, then make a circus hitch by wrapping the cable around itself four times out and three times back.

The whole thing takes less than fifteen seconds. Damn,

if the judges could see me now! I might not be the best actor, but I would definitely win the stagecraft competition.

Now if the killer tries to follow me back to the common room, he'll go sprawling.

As I jump to my feet, a flashlight pins me in place. "Stop right there!" a voice barks.

In shock, I spin around. It's Stuart. He's alive!

Dressed all in black, Stuart's in a half crouch, hands at chest height, wrists crossed. His left hand holds a small flashlight, and his left wrist supports his right hand, which holds a gun. Stuart looks just as shocked as I do. "Nell? What—what are you doing?"

"Oh my God, you're alive!" I feel limp with relief. Not only is Stuart alive, now he can be in charge. I haven't seen any flames yet, but the hazy cone of light reveals just how thick the smoke is becoming. "We were sure that cougar killed you."

"It did take a good chunk out of me. I'm just lucky I was wearing so many layers. I think it got frustrated, or maybe it was just caching me for later. All I know is I woke up under some bushes in the dark. I managed to make it back here and bandaged myself up. Then I smelled smoke and came out to investigate." His voice hardens. "So what are you doing out here, Nell? And why are there ashes all over your face? Did you start the fire?"

Stuart can't seriously think I did it. Right? But then why is his gun still trained on me?

In sputtering sentences that sound confusing even to me, I try to explain everything as fast as possible. Finding the family in the truck. Spending the night in the barricaded common room. The alcohol that must have been drugged. Waking to the smell of two kinds of gas. Grabbing the luggage trolley. Stumbling across Linus's body. I end with, "Edgar or Brian must be trying to kill everybody."

"You gotta admit, that's a pretty crazy story," Stuart says slowly. But while he says it, he slips the gun into the back of his waistband. "Since I never made it to the police station, we're on our own. Even if someone spots the smoke, it's going to take a long time for the fire department to make it out here." He beckons. "Come on. There are some fire extinguishers in the guest wing. Maybe if you help me, it won't be too late to put it out."

The word *fire* reminds me of the red foam I saw in his wastebasket. The piece that looked like the drawing of a campfire. Suddenly I realize I should have been looking at the negative space, like when someone first shows you the arrow in the middle of the FedEx logo. It wasn't a campfire or a throwing star.

I should have looked at what wasn't there. What had been cut out was the paw print of a cougar.

My thoughts are interrupted by noise and light. When I turn, Adam, Jermaine, and Travis are running toward us. Adam carries the old rifle. Travis has the cast-iron frying pan. Jermaine has a cell phone in flashlight mode in one hand and the rolling pin in the other. When they see Stuart, they skid to a stop about ten feet behind me.

"Stuart!" Travis's voice is filled with joy. "Are you okay?"

"I got a few chunks missing, a little bit of frostbite here and there, but I got lucky, buddy."

"Stuart actually managed to survive getting attacked by the cougar," I say. "Adam, I can't wait to tell Judge Wargrave when we get home. You know he loves those wilderness adventure stories."

"Judge War—" Adam starts to echo, then falls silent. Does he remember that Judge Wargrave is a character in *And Then There Were None*?

In the play, the judge kills everyone, faking his own death along the way.

Just as I think Stuart is planning.

38

ONE MORE CHANCE

Sunday, 6:58 AM

"STUART, LOOK!" TRAVIS CRIES. "THE GUEST ROOMS MUST BE ON fire!"

While he's speaking, Adam starts circling Stuart. Stuart turns on his heel to face him just as Adam raises the rifle and points it directly at Stuart's chest.

"You're lying," Adam says. There's no doubt in his voice.

Stuart's exaggerated laugh would never pass muster with Mrs. McElroy. "You do know that thing doesn't work?"

Adam shifts his hands on the barrel, instantly turning it into a club.

What happens next is a blur. Adam steps forward and swings the rifle at Stuart's head. But Stuart is already darting out of range and toward me. As he does, his flashlight bounces away, landing to face the pool. Then he wraps his left arm around my neck and presses the barrel of his pistol against my temple.

At the touch of the cold circle against my skin, I freeze. We all do.

"And I can assure you, my gun definitely works," Stuart says as he angles me to face the others. The Tiger's Tail and the pool are behind us. Adam is on our left. Jermaine and Travis are to our right. So is the cable, only a few feet away. Jermaine is shaking so hard his phone flashlight is trembling, bouncing on my face and then away.

"Don't hurt her," Adam says.

"If you don't want that to happen, then all of you put down that stuff you took off the walls."

Adam lays down the rifle, and Jermaine sets down the rolling pin.

Travis drops the cast-iron frying pan. In a shaky voice, he says, "Travis doesn't understand what's going on." The sentence ends with a cough. The smoke is thickening from tendrils to a mist.

"Stuart's the killer," I say. "He must have killed Jade and Gary. He killed Maeve and Valeria. And now he wants to kill us."

Travis nervously rakes his fingers through his goatee. "That can't be true."

"The newspaper article you read us said things were missing from Jade and Gary," I say. "Do you know what things?"

"Gary's wedding ring. And one of Jade's dangly earrings. Gold with blue stones."

"Check out the cigar box in Stuart's bathroom. I think they're in there, along with a lot of other women's jewelry."

Stuart pulls his hand back from my shoulder so he can stroke one finger along the gold chain around my neck. "Gosh, I wonder what I'll take from you, Blondie?" The nickname is a deliberate echo of Maeve. I try not to shiver in disgust. Out of the corner of my eye I see Stuart's grin. "Although you know what they say—you never forget your first."

It seems impossible. But Stuart sounds nostalgic.

"It wasn't the bartender Jade argued with that night. It was me. The place was hopping, and he needed an extra pair of hands to help bus. She walked in already drunk. When he wouldn't serve her, she tried flirting with me. After I said I wouldn't help her, she called me a snot-nosed kid and flounced out.

"The more I thought about it, the madder I got. So later I left with the bar knife and a bottle of Maker's Mark. After I got the master key, I knocked on their door. I said

I'd brought something to apologize. I gave her one more chance, but she didn't thank me or anything. Just kept saying her boyfriend was asleep, and then closed the door right in my face." Stuart's tone is edged with remembered annoyance.

"So I waited a bit and used the key to get in. They were both asleep. I killed him first. And let me tell you, by then Jade was finally willing to pay attention to me. But it was too late."

Travis makes a sad, small groan.

"After they were dead I pulled up the chair and just looked at them. It was amazing. I knew I wasn't a child anymore. A child couldn't do what I'd done. I was a man."

As Stuart's been talking, his grip on me has been loosening. The arm that was looped around my chest is now just across my back. But I'm only going to get one chance to try to do anything.

"I think my parents guessed, because suddenly they claimed the local high school wasn't good enough. They sent me to a military academy. Afterward, I went into the service." He grimaces. "But the army didn't understand me, either. After I was discharged I started driving long-haul trucks. It's a good job for someone like me. Someone who has a certain . . . itch."

Reframing an early conversation, I interrupt his monologue. "Travis said that sometimes you talk about the one who got away. But you didn't mean a girlfriend, did you?"

252

"You're not as dumb as you look, Blondie." He squeezes my shoulder. "Stupid girl ran off into the woods and I couldn't find her." He huffs in annoyance. "I made sure that never happened again. After my folks died, I came back here and tried to go straight. Do bad things where you live, it's easier for the cops to figure out. When the urge gets too strong, I put Travis in charge for the night and go for a long drive. Pick the right people—runaways, homeless, prostitutes—no one ever looks for them. No one cares."

The pressure of the gun against my temple has eased.

"People like Travis," Travis says softly.

Stuart's chuckle ends in a cough. "Just thank your lucky stars you're not my type. But Jade and Gary were special. And then you kids showed up. I even told you about what I'd done, but you acted like death was a joke. Playing with the Ouija board, pretending you were talking to them. And worst of all, those two stupid girls pretended to be dead. So they had to be taught a lesson."

"But it wasn't even their idea," Jermaine objects. "Dev told us that Knox blackmailed them."

Stuart shrugs, unfazed.

"And then you faked your own death," I say. "You made us think it was the cougar."

"Very good, Blondie. I cut cat prints out of the back of a pair of old flip-flops and then glued the pieces on the front half of the sole. With them, a piece torn off my coat, and the fake blood I confiscated from the girls, it wasn't hard to make you believe in something you were already afraid of. Then I picked my way down the creek and made it back here. From the basement, you can hear pretty much anything."

"You spiked that bottle we found," Adam says, waving the smoke away from his face. It's starting to fill the concourse like fog.

"I figured you wouldn't be able to resist, so I crushed up sleeping pills and found a bottle of something god-awful. I also slipped some crushed-up pills in the lemonade Travis likes, and in Edgar's whiskey and Brian's Coke. When I was finishing up, I ran into Linus coming back from his car with his little secret. That money was like a sign I was doing the right thing. Then when everybody was asleep, I went down to the basement, came up through the kitchen, and turned on the gas. This place is insured. It's worth more as a heap of smoking rubble than as a going concern."

My breath shakes when I inhale. I don't even try to act like I'm not afraid. In fact, I amplify it. "You're going to make it look like an accident. Like the power went out and we all got trapped by a fire when we were trying to keep warm."

"Not just a fire," he says. "Once the flames meet the natural gas, everything's going to go boom."

There's a flaw in Stuart's plan, one that might save us. "But if you shoot us, they'll find the bullets in our bodies and know it's no accident."

I feel his shrug. "The military teaches you that no plan survives contact with the enemy. I'll just tell them Edgar was drunk and threatening people."

Now that his boasting is over, he'll kill us. Is there any way I can make him lower his guard? "Please, please don't hurt us," I beg hysterically, mentally calculating the distance between him and the trip wire.

"Don't worry, Blondie." His voice is honeyed. "It'll be over fast."

Travis clears his throat. "What about Travis, Stu?"

He grunts. "I guess that's up to you."

"What you done is wrong." Travis's voice trembles.

"Okay, you've made your bed," Stuart says, but Travis looks confused. I don't think Travis understands he just signed his own death warrant.

If I'm going to act, it has to be now. Before Stuart makes a move. Before the fire catches up with the fumes.

I strengthen my voice. "In the theater world, we have our own sayings to guide us, right, guys? Like, 'All the world's a stage, and all the men and women merely players. They have their exits'—Adam, stage right! Jermaine, house out!"

The moment that follows seems like an eternity, but it's really only a split second. If Adam moves to his right—not ours—he'll be less likely to get shot. And *house out* is the command the stage manager gives to cut the house lights.

Jermaine at least gets it, because his phone flashlight

immediately goes out, plunging us into near darkness. The only light is from Stuart's fallen flashlight shining toward the pool.

I shove my shoulder as hard as I can into the side of his chest, just as my right arm swims up and around his right arm. The arm with the gun. At the same time my left hand grabs the barrel and pushes it up.

My shove sends Stuart tumbling over the wire. As he does, the gun goes off. *Crack!* The bullet whizzes past my ear and hits the ceiling

The ceiling that I now see is on fire.

I leap over the trip wire and jump on top of Stuart, landing as hard as I can, my hands scrabbling for the gun. "Help me!" I scream. The sound is muffled in my right ear. "Help me get the gun!"

A voice booms out of the darkness that leads to the foyer. "Stuart! Give me back my damn money." It's Linus, with his southern drawl.

Linus, who lies dead in the lobby.

The world seems to pause a beat while we all try to process this information.

And then it's a tangle of bodies as Jermaine, Adam, and Travis converge on us. Stuart grunts as he is kicked and hit. I don't escape unscathed. A foot connects with my ribs. A blow hits the side of my head, making my other ear ring.

Suddenly Travis yells, "I got it!"

Stuart and I both scramble to our feet.

I realize I can see Stuart, at least a little bit. Not just from the breaking dawn, but from the flames rolling over our heads.

A burning ceiling tile drops on the dusty palm fronds of the Tiger's Tail's roof. Suddenly the tiki bar is lighting up like a torch. The flames race down the wooden support beams.

A flaming frond lands on Jermaine's shirt. With a shriek he bats at it, but now his shirt is on fire. He runs to the edge of the pool and jumps in. While the water immediately douses the flames, he starts thrashing in the water. Panicking. Remembering he can't swim, I race over and dive in next to him.

And almost break my outstretched arms. The water is only about four feet deep.

I get my feet under me and reach for him. "Jermaine! Stand up!"

He does. More and more debris is falling into the water. Pretty soon this entire area will be on fire, and I don't trust the swimming pool to help us survive. Not when the air we need to breathe will be superheated. Even now, every breath is like leaning into an oven.

The whole concourse is alight. Not just from the ceiling, but from flames that have begun to eat their way along the carpet, back toward the lobby.

Worse yet, Stuart is fighting Travis for the gun. Travis breaks free, but he's smaller and older than the other man.

Behind them, the Tiger's Tail is collapsing on itself, hollowed out by fire.

"Watch out!" I yell. "It's coming down!"

Travis backs away, but Stuart shakes his head. "You're not a good enough actor to carry that off, Blondie."

His laugh is turned into screams as he is swallowed by the flames.

39

DOLLS GOD GOT TIRED OF

Sunday, 7:25 AM

"No!"

Travis starts forward, hands outstretched and mouth open. His shriek is so loud and full of pain he must be denying it all: Stuart being a killer. Stuart planning on letting Travis die along with everyone else. Stuart being swallowed up by the flames.

For a moment, Stuart is a human torch, but then another heap of burning rubble collapses. Mercifully we can no longer see him.

Meanwhile, under a rain of burning debris that sizzles when it hits the water, Adam helps Jermaine and me scramble out of the pool. With the wet hem of my sweater, I wipe the ashes from my face.

A shout behind us is louder even than the roar and crackle of the flames. At first I don't recognize the man staggering toward us from the back of the motel. It's Edgar. Half his hair is burned off, and his face is smudged with soot, but he's alive.

"Where is Stuart?" he yells. "I caught him lighting the rooms on fire!"

Travis points at the flaming wreckage that used to be the Tiger's Tail. "Somewhere in there." His voice breaks. "He's gone, Edgar." He looks at the gun in his hand and then suddenly pitches it into the flames.

"Come on!" Adam waves in the direction of the lobby. "We need to make sure everyone is out of the common room before the fire gets there. That gas could still explode."

We half run, half stagger down the concourse. And then we spot Dev running toward us. I realize how Linus managed to talk to us. It was really Dev, trying to buy us a moment's distraction. He must have overheard what Stuart said.

"Come on, guys!" He points toward the parking lot. "Everyone else took blankets and went out to Brian's truck. I came looking for you and heard enough from Stuart that I tried to throw a wrench in the works. But now we've got to get out of here."

With each step we put a little more distance between us and the fire. For the moment, at least, we are outpacing it.

But Edgar is burned, I've got only one shoe, and Jermaine and I are both soaked, our pants so heavy with water we occasionally have to yank them up midstride.

Dev races out the double doors, Edgar on his heels.

I start after them, but Adam puts his hand on my arm.

"You guys will freeze to death in those wet clothes, and Nell, you need a shoe. Let's get you changed and then get the hell out of here and into the truck. The fire's going to reach this part of the motel soon, and we don't want to still be here when that happens. A natural gas explosion could turn this place into a pile of kindling."

"But what about the girls?" Travis asks, his eyes wild. "Are you just going to leave them?"

Jermaine grabs his arm. "What girls?"

I feel a pulse of hope. "Do you mean Maeve and Valeria?"

He nods. "Travis thinks he knows where they are."

"What?" Adam says. "Where?"

He points toward his feet. "In the basement."

"Do you mean their bodies?" I ask, thinking about how Stuart came up from the basement to turn on the gas. "Or are they alive?"

"There were noises last night."

Adam, Jermaine, and I trade glances, but we already know we can't take the chance of leaving them behind. Instead we set out at a run for the common room. We dig through the other team's suitcases to find something—anything—we can change into. I'm pretty sure it's Knox's clothes that I dress in, all of us facing the wall to give the illusion of privacy.

A minute later, we follow Travis into the kitchen. He shoves aside the shelving unit that's blocking the door and then goes down the stairs. We follow his phone flashlight down. He walks to the back of the pantry and then enters a dark hall so narrow that our shoulders brush against the rough walls as we move.

We pass through spaces that look like they came from a nightmare. Rotting insulation lying in pink tufts on the ground, falling-apart pool furniture red with rust, heaps of gray mattresses destroyed by mice.

We end up in a place I recognize. The equally creepy boiler room. I orient myself. Travis's workspace must be directly above us. As I'm thinking that, he slips between two giant metal tanks, and we all follow. The space behind the tanks is only about six feet wide, just a long wall made of gray cinder blocks mortared together with white cement. I think we're facing the parking lot. The only thing back here is a wooden shelving unit holding various tools as well as bits and pieces of equipment, none of which I recognize. It's only after Travis gets on one side of the shelves and begins to push that I see the outline of a door behind it, nearly invisible and marked out by slightly thicker lines of mortar.

"What's in there?" Adam asks as he and Jermaine help shove the shelves the rest of the way.

"An old bomb shelter." Travis sets his hand into a gap and pulls. The door swings back, revealing that the cinder blocks were mortared to a piece of plywood. His flashlight moves from left to right, revealing a space about the size of one of the motel rooms. Inside are two folding chairs, shelves holding canned goods so old they should be in a museum, and three crumbling cardboard boxes labeled CANNED WATER. On the right-hand side is a set of wooden bunk beds topped with thin blue plastic mattresses.

Maeve lies on the bottom bunk and Valeria on the top. They are absolutely unmoving, flat on their backs, their arms neat by their sides. They look like dolls that God got tired of playing with and put away. My chest feels as if someone just reached in, put a fist around my heart, and squeezed.

Crying out, "Jesus, no!" Jermaine jumps over the threshold and runs to the bunk beds. He reaches up to grab the hand of one girl, and then leans down to grab the other.

The rest of us follow, quietly, as if reluctant to wake them, even though it's clear they're not simply asleep. The only light comes from Travis's phone.

So when I see the smallest of movements, I'm not sure if it's real. Did Valeria's hand just twitch?

"Wait," I say, or start to.

Because then the world explodes.

40

CLOSER AND CLOSER
Seven weeks later
Saturday, 8:37 PM

As THE CLAPPING SWELLS, A RED ROSE LANDS AT MY FEET. Letting go of Adam's hand, I lean down to pick it up from the stage. With a grin, I put it between my teeth. The stem is stiff and grassy-tasting. Grinning even wider in case there are thorns, I grab Adam's hand again for another bow.

The entire audience is on their feet. Front-row center are our drama club's guests of honor: Oscar, Knox, Dev, Maeve, and Valeria.

Maeve and Valeria weren't dead, just drugged. After discovering the two girls hiding in the conference room, Stuart had marched them at gunpoint down to the old bomb shelter. Knowing the blizzard would both provide a cover story and hinder any investigation, he decided to destroy the business he could not save and make it look like an accident. Since killing them outright might have tipped the police that things weren't what they seemed, he forced Maeve and Valeria to take large doses of Ambien. The theory was that after drugging us and starting the fire, Stuart had planned to drag their limp forms upstairs.

The explosion turned much of the motel into matchsticks. But the old fallout shelter saved us, and Brian's truck saved the rest. Even Brian survived. Waking to flames in the hall, he had jumped from the second floor, his fall cushioned by the deep snow. He then took refuge in his own truck.

Edgar has recovered from his burns. And while he is still working as a pharmaceutical rep, he's started attending a recovery program for addicts.

Now Brian's in jail, awaiting trial for human trafficking. Reuben and Consuela helped immigration sever the tentacles of the network he worked for. In return, the Salazar family has received special visas that allow them to live and work in the US, and to eventually apply for green cards.

When authorities combed the wreckage, they found only a few singed bills from Linus's bank robbery. They figure it mostly burned up or turned into confetti. Linus had said he was going to visit his mother, and it turns out that part was actually true. Now he's buried about twenty miles from where he died.

The money may have been destroyed, but the cigar box tucked in Stuart's bathroom drawer survived, cracked but intact. The FBI is still trying to match each ring and necklace he kept as a souvenir to the victim it represents. They're looking at missing-person reports, talking to families, and even retrieving tiny amounts of DNA off some pieces. Besides Gary and Jade, as well as Linus, so far Stuart's been linked to five other murders in four states. And it turns out that he hadn't left the military voluntarily. He had been dishonorably discharged after being suspected of killing Iraqi civilians.

Travis, hailed as a hero, was offered a job as a janitor in the next town over. A GoFundMe we started generated enough money for him to rent and furnish a small apartment.

Next to me, Min lets go of my hand for a moment to wave at Valeria. She's not quite forgiven her for taking part in Knox's "prank," but she's keeping an open mind. Knox had forced Valeria to play along by threatening to tell her traditional parents that she's gay. When she got home, she told them herself. Turns out not to have been a big surprise.

As for me, I still can't believe I was cast in the lead role. For the first time in my life, I wasn't too scared to try out for it.

In the wings, Mrs. McElroy is clapping her hands off and looking right at me. I see her mouth, "Brava!"

On the other end of the line, Jermaine and Raven are bowing with their arms around each other's waists. Surviving a near-death experience has cemented their relationship. Now if you see one, you know the other can't be more than a few feet away. As a result, Raven is a little calmer and Jermaine a little looser.

And Adam and me? Well, being cast as the leads has meant we have spent nearly every hour together, at least when we're not in class or asleep. Running lines, blocking moves, and talking, talking, talking. About favorite books, the best music, and what we want to do when we graduate next year.

But that's all we've been doing. Talking. We have been sitting closer and closer, touching each other's wrists and shoulders, and last night after final dress rehearsal we even got into a tickle fight. We still haven't kissed. I'm starting to wonder if we ever will and telling myself I should just be happy we're friends.

Besides, right now, as I hold his hand and grin at the standing ovation, I feel on top of the world.

And just as I am thinking this, Adam plucks the rose from between my teeth with a flourish. Then he pulls me to him and puts his lips on mine.

The cheers fade away. There's nothing but the feel of his lips on mine, soft and hard at once. His hands rest on either side of my jaw, then slip into my hair. The kiss takes me into another world. It shows me that those kisses I got in seventh grade were nothing.

When we finally separate, the clapping is at a crescendo, accompanied by whooping and hollering. But Adam only has eyes for me, and me for him.

"What are you looking at?" he teases.

"It's like you said in the car on the way to the competition," I say.

"What?"

I grin. "Look where you want to go."

ACKNOWLEDGMENTS

TWO TRUTHS AND A LIE MARKS MY FIRST BOOK WITH LITTLE, Brown—and my twelfth with my editor Christy Ottaviano! She has the uncanny ability to find the heart of every book. Her insight and unflagging support always inspire me to dig a little deeper.

My agent, Wendy Schmalz, has carefully guided my career for nearly thirty books, and become one of my oldest friends in the process.

In a world where editors and agents come and go, I've been incredibly lucky to have two wonderful mentors for so long. I'm so proud of what we have created together.

The entire team at Little, Brown has been truly amazing, including Karina Granda, Mara Brashem, Andie Divelbiss, Bill Grace, Victoria Stapleton, Sydney Tillman, Marisa Finkelstein, Sarah Chassé, Regina Castillo, and Lillian Sun.

This book was written during the pandemic, and, oh, how I missed seeing the YA community in person: readers, authors, bloggers, teachers, librarians, booksellers, and festival volunteers. Nothing against Zoom, but I can't wait to see you all in real life again.

A special thanks to all the readers who chimed in on Twitter and Facebook when I was stuck for just the right name or detail.

So many people helped me pull this book together. Any errors are my own.

Tracy Nunnally, owner of Vertigo (getvertigo.com), is a world-renowned expert in flying effects and theatrical rigging. He has done everything from "flying" a bullet in a movie to flying a huge pickup over a packed stadium. Early in the pandemic we had a FaceTime conversation where he demonstrated how to create a theatrical hanging using what he had handy: his phone charging cord and a bottle of Hershey's syrup. He answered many questions and even sent me photos from his shop to explain exactly how things work.

Jeremy W. Floyd, a costume designer and an expert on all things theater, helped me with both musical lyrics and a bunch of weird questions about stage blood.

After watching actor Melanie Neu in *Thespians,* a documentary about a regional high school theater competition, I managed to track her down in Italy. Both the documentary and Melanie helped me understand a world I left when I was sixteen. She is still a working actor.

Theater geek and mystery writer Cindy Brown gave me advice about the wonderful world of drama.

Cathy Humble helped me with Latin translations.

Professor Rachel Lance, PhD, of Duke University, is an expert in blast trauma—and also gave me some hints on how to make things go boom.

Lee Etten, a fire captain and paramedic at Portland Fire & Rescue, gave me advice on fire behavior.

Paul Dreyer, CEO of Avid4 Adventure (avid4.com), which introduces kids to the powers of the outdoors, answered my questions about how to treat hypothermia.

Mark Berger, CEO of Securitech, helped me figure out how to keep doors closed that should be open and doors open that should be closed.

Randy Patten

APRIL HENRY

is the *New York Times* bestselling author of many acclaimed mysteries for adults and young adults, including the YA novels *Girl, Stolen*; *The Night She Disappeared*; *The Girl Who Was Supposed to Die*; *The Girl I Used to Be*, which was nominated for an Edgar Award and won the Anthony Award for Best YA Mystery; *Count All Her Bones*; *The Lonely Dead*; *Run, Hide, Fight Back*; *The Girl in the White Van*; *Playing with Fire*; *Eyes of the Forest*; and *The Body in the Woods* and *Blood Will Tell*, the first two books in the Point Last Seen series. She lives in Oregon. April invites you to visit her at aprilhenry.com.